# "You Were There Long Enough To Acquire A Lover,"

Flynn reminded her gently, his tawny eyes gleaming.

Heather felt the warmth rush into her face, but she kept her voice cool. "No, Flynn. I dated one of the owners of the company, but there was no love involved. I never had a *lover* while I was working at ConStruct. I got used."

Flynn's jaw tightened. He was aware of the prowling tension in himself and the wariness in Heather. He'd known it wasn't going to be easy. He'd known she wouldn't run back into his arms. He'd told himself to be realistic. But for the first time, Flynn faced the reality of the task that lay ahead of him. He'd burned her badly, and she wasn't going to willingly risk returning to the source of the fire.

Dear Reader,

Welcome to Silhouette! Our goal is to give you hours of unbeatable reading pleasure, and we hope you'll enjoy each month's six new Silhouette Desires. These sensual, provocative love stories are both believable and compelling—sometimes they're poignant, sometimes humorous, but always enjoyable.

Indulge yourself. Experience all the passion and excitement of falling in love along with our heroine as she meets the irresistible man of her dreams and together they overcome all obstacles in the path to a happy ending.

If this is your first Desire, I hope it'll be the first of many. If you're already a Silhouette Desire reader, thanks for your support! Look for some of your favorite authors in the coming months: Stephanie James, Diana Palmer, Dixie Browning, Ann Major and Doreen Owens Malek, to name just a few.

Happy reading!

Isabel Swift
Senior Editor

SDRL-7/85

# STEPHANIE JAMES
## Second Wife

Silhouette Desire

Published by Silhouette Books New York

**America's Publisher of Contemporary Romance**

SILHOUETTE BOOKS
300 East 42nd St., New York, N.Y. 10017

Copyright © 1986 by Jayne Krentz Inc.

ISBN: 0-373-05307-X

First Silhouette Books printing October 1986

America's Publisher of Contemporary Romance

Printed in the U.S.A.

---

## *STEPHANIE JAMES*

readily admits that the chief influence on her writing is her "lifelong addiction to romantic daydreaming." She has spent the past nine years living and working with her engineer husband in a wide variety of places, including the Caribbean, the Southeast and the Pacific Northwest. Ms. James also writes under the name Jayne Krentz and Jayne Castle.

# One

He stood on the sidewalk in front of her house, feeling as grim and resolute as if he were going into battle. The analogy was far too apt.

There was always the outside possibility his sweet enemy would take one look at him, throw herself into his arms and surrender without firing a shot. But Flynn Rammage didn't waste much time tantalizing himself with that false hope. It was highly unlikely things were going to be that simple, not after what he'd done to her eight months ago. Maybe he didn't deserve to have it that easy.

Eight months ago he'd been too embittered and too filled with rage to realize what Heather Devaney was offering. He'd seen gentleness and mistaken it for weakness. She'd offered love and Flynn had seen vulnerability. He'd been a wolf on the hunt and Heather had been the unwary victim.

Eight months ago he'd been a fool, Flynn told himself. He'd thrown away gold because he hadn't been searching for it. He'd been looking for a target and Heather had gotten in his way. She had become the target.

Flynn took a deep breath of the warm evening air and started up the walk to the front door of a small, shabby house. It was hard to imagine Heather in such a place. Weeds choked what was left of the lawn. There were cracks in the pavement that led to the steps. The screen door was loose on its hinges, the wire mesh ruptured in several places. The whole house badly needed a coat of paint.

Flynn automatically surveyed the modest little bungalow with an expert's eye. He wouldn't have bet fifty cents on the soundness of the structure, and he could just imagine the condition of the electrical wiring. What in hell had made Heather leave her cheerful little apartment and move in here?

Overhead the Tucson sky was filled with stars, however, and in spite of the physical condition of the house, he knew it belonged to Heather. Flynn was grateful to have finally run her to ground. The lights in the windows of Heather's home, wherever it was and whatever condition it was in, would always promise warmth and love and happiness. She carried those qualities within herself. They were all items Flynn had been missing for a long time. He was prepared to fight to regain them.

Heather Devaney shook off the faint trickle of uneasy awareness she'd experienced more than once during the day and flung open another closet door. Her imagination had been unusually active all afternoon for some reason. More than once she'd stopped a cleaning project to walk over to a window and glance outside. There had been nothing to see, of course, just the quiet residential street in front of her new home. She didn't understand why she had a vague feeling of being watched. It annoyed her, but it didn't really alarm her. This was a good neighborhood even if it was a little run-down, and she was delighted to have finally taken possession of her house. She wasn't going to allow an overactive imagination to upset her on her first night in the place.

She eyed the dust balls inside the closet with an air of undaunted determination. The real estate agent had promised the house would be thoroughly cleaned before she took possession, but it was clear his notion of a clean home differed from her own.

It didn't matter, Heather decided as she closed the closet and went across the room to take a closer look at some marks on the wall. She was going to have the rooms repainted, anyway, and when that was done she could do a proper cleaning. Tonight she would concentrate on the bathroom and kitchen. At least all the appliances worked, she reminded herself cheerfully. Considering their age, that was saying something.

She leaned down to study the wall marks and came to the conclusion they represented the artistic endeavors of a three-year-old. Not bad, really. A slight leaning toward minimalism, but a nice sense of color and line. The kid had promise.

For a moment Heather allowed herself to dwell on the image of a child playing in the house. Then, with a faintly wistful expression, she straightened and reached out to touch the sagging drapes. No doubt about it, they would have to be replaced. Just as well.

She didn't like the beige shade, and the fabric struck her as heavy-looking for a home in the desert. Heather wanted the crisp look of miniblinds for this room. It was going to be her guest room.

She released the handful of drapery and walked out into the hall with a deep feeling of satisfaction. A home of her own. It was a small place, a tiny two-bedroom bungalow in the charming southwestern style, with arching doorways and a mock adobe look. True, it needed a lot of work, but it was the first place she had ever owned, and it was hers alone. Every last mortgage payment. She grinned to herself and sauntered into the kitchen.

There was a bottle of wine on the old tile counter, a nice pizza red that was waiting for the arrival of the pizza and Heather's guest. She considered helping herself to a sip or two while she waited for Lee. He was late.

Heather was still deliberating the matter, when the knock came on the door.

"Got to remember to get the doorbell fixed," she murmured to herself as she hurried into the small front room. She didn't bother glancing through the peep-hole. It could only be Lee Osborne, and he would have his hands full of pizza. Heather yanked open the door, a laughing smile on her face. "I hope you remembered the anchovies and the hot peppers. I need sustenance—"

The smile froze on her face and in her eyes as she saw who stood on the threshold.

"Hello, Heather," Flynn Rammage said.

For one endless instant Heather couldn't believe it. The world seemed to tilt slightly, just enough to jar everything loose. When things resettled they were in a slightly different position. Heather felt as if she'd opened the wrong door or stepped into the wrong film. Her first instinct was to close the door and try again. Then reality realigned itself. Heather forced herself to adjust to it.

"Hello, Flynn." She kept the smile in place, but the warmth had gone out of it. "What in the world are you doing here? I thought you were on some construction project in Saudi Arabia."

"My job there is finished. I'm home."

Heather shook her head, her smile turning wryly amused. "Not quite. Your house is about ten miles in that direction." She gestured vaguely toward the night-shrouded foothills behind him. She had never been there, but she knew the approximate location. "This is my home." She heard the faint challenge underlying her words and decided not to worry about it. It was true that Flynn reacted naturally to challenges, but she could and would defend herself. Besides, she was a householder now, and householders had certain rights. Perhaps she'd see about getting a large dog.

"Aren't you going to invite me in?"

"Should I?" she asked blandly.

"I'd like to talk to you."

"I think you said enough eight months ago, Flynn."

"All the wrong things."

Heather looked at him, using all her energy to keep her expression as serenely polite as possible. "I'm afraid I really don't have time to chat just now, Flynn. This is my first night in my new home and I've got a ton of things to do. I'm sure you understand what I mean when I say that at the moment I've got a list of priorities and you're not on it."

She thought his tawny eyes hardened, but it might have been just a trick of the porch light. The slight smile that edged Flynn's hard mouth didn't waver.

"If that's a subtle way of reminding me that I had my priorities screwed up a few months back, you don't have to bother. I'm well aware of it. May I come in, Heather?"

"Why?" she asked bluntly.

"I want to talk to you."

"Why?" she asked again.

He studied her for a long moment. "You're not going to make this easy for me, are you?"

"Make what easy?" Her bewilderment was real. "Flynn, I haven't got the faintest idea of what you want, but I'm quite sure that whatever it is, I don't intend to give it to you. Not this time. So why don't you just hop back into your fancy Porsche and drive off into the sunset? I'm expecting someone at any moment and I'd rather not have to explain you to him."

"I'll explain myself to him." Flynn slid one booted foot over the threshold and calmly moved into the small front hall. He glanced around the bare living room. "Who is he? Anyone I know?"

"I doubt it. Flynn, I'm asking you to leave." Heather kept her voice level and calm as he shouldered his way past her. Above all she must not lose her temper or her nerve. Flynn Rammage was very good at homing in on any sign of weakness.

"It took me quite a while to find you, Heather." He ignored her request for him to leave. "No one seemed to know where you'd gone after you quit your job a few months ago." Flynn wandered across the living room, examining the worn carpet and the marked walls with a mildly critical eye. The furniture was limited to a rickety-looking card table, some folding chairs and a stereo. Heather's collection of records was housed in a cardboard box.

"I didn't see any reason to post a notice giving my new address." Heather remained where she was in the hall, letting the front door stand open. She folded her arms under her breasts and leaned nonchalantly against the wall, as if Flynn's intrusion were a minor but rather boorish breach of good manners.

He turned to look at her and the faint smile on his face suddenly warmed his eyes. Heather stared at him with deep distrust. He looked very much as he had eight months ago. Rammage was thirty-eight years old, his body tough and lean from the outdoor work he did. In spite of her best intentions, there had been times during the past eight months when Heather had found herself remembering the feel of Flynn's solid strength against her. She had always been very good at fantasizing. So good, in fact, that she had occasionally fooled herself where Flynn was concerned.

His dark-brown hair was a little shorter now. It looked as though it had recently been cut. There were a few more sprinkles of silver in it, but the rakish wave was still there—the one that refused to be tamed by a barber's razor or a woman's fingers. The lines of his face hadn't softened any in the past few months. Heather had a hunch they never would. The jagged blade of a nose, the high, broad cheekbones and the implacable jaw were all permanent fixtures in a face that stopped short of being ugly but went much too far in another, more dangerous direction. There had always been an intrinsic, relentless hardness in that face. Heather shuddered to remember her own foolishness in thinking she could reach through the hardness to touch the vulnerable man she had been so certain lay below.

Flynn was wearing the boots, jeans and casual work shirt he had favored when Heather had first met him. The two partners who owned Con-Struct International were as different as night and day. Sam Erickson was the polished, brilliant salesman who was good at lining up contracts and keeping clients happy. Heather remembered he had always dressed the part; his pinstripe suits were legendary in the halls of the firm's main offices in Tucson.

But Flynn Rammage was the site man, the hard-driving, frequently ruthless boss who went out on the projects when there was trouble and who made sure the problems got fixed, regardless of whose head rolled in the process. Rammage had a reputation for doing whatever it took to bring a construction job in on time and underbudget. The amazing thing was that he did it without alienating the men who worked for him. Rammage's abilities had generated their own legends. He saw no need to bother with pinstripe suits, and as far as Heather knew, no one had ever tried to stuff him into one. Except, perhaps, his ex-wife. Irritably Heather put thoughts of the unknown woman out of her mind.

"Why did you make such a secret out of the new job, Heather?" Flynn asked.

Heather managed a small, careless shrug. "I didn't figure anyone at Con-Struct International particularly cared where the new manager of central files went. I wasn't at Con-Struct long enough to develop any good friends."

"You were there long enough to acquire a lover," Flynn reminded her gently, tawny eyes gleaming.

Heather felt the warmth rush to her face, but she kept her voice cool. "No, Flynn. I got laid by one of the owners of the company, but there was no love involved. I never had a *lover* while I was working at Con-Struct. I got used."

Flynn's jaw tightened. He was aware of the prowling tension in himself and the wariness in Heather. He'd known it wasn't going to be easy. He'd known she wouldn't run back into his arms. He'd told himself to be realistic. But for the first time Flynn faced the reality of the task that lay ahead of him. He'd burned her badly and she wasn't going to willingly risk returning to the source of the fire.

As he stood watching her Flynn felt his body tighten with desire. Restlessly he shifted position in a useless attempt to ease the hunger in himself. He had to stay in control, or the war was lost before it even began. Flynn groaned inwardly. Eight months of wanting had built into a powerful need that wasn't going to be easily governed.

She still wore her hair in that loose, easy twist at the back of her head. Flynn was glad she hadn't cut it. Most of the women he knew who were thirty years old wore their hair in short, sassy styles that were chic but lacked the primitive sensuality of long hair. There had been too many nights when he'd lain awake remembering the sweet scent of the brown-blond mass of Heather's hair and the way it had cascaded softly around her shoulders when he'd unpinned the casual knot.

Heather was thinner than Flynn remembered. She had always been slender, but now her waist was really tiny. The delicacy of it emphasized the curve of her small breasts and gently flaring thighs. He wondered if she'd lost weight because of what he'd done to her. Was it wishful, egotistical thinking on his part to want to believe he'd had that much effect on her? There was no denying the fact that the fine lines of her face seemed a little more sharply etched.

Her hazel eyes were still Heather's most riveting feature. Deeply fringed, wide and faintly tilted at the outer corners, Heather's eyes had once held all the warmth and feminine welcome in the world for Flynn. He had reached out to take all of that warmth and welcome and had used it to feed the unquenchable fury that had raged within him. Even as he remembered what he'd done and relived his own self-disgust, Flynn knew he wanted Heather more than ever.

He ran his eyes over her, vividly aware of the way the snug, faded jeans emphasized her sweetly shaped derriere. She had on a brilliant fuchsia shirt that made her look like a bright wildflower that had been plucked and brought into the house. Flynn wondered what she would do if he simply walked back across the room and took her into his arms.

"I was a bastard eight months ago, Heather."

She blinked owlishly. "I'll go along with that."

"I've changed."

"In just eight months? I doubt it."

Flynn sighed, prowling to the opposite end of the small room. He looked out the window. "There were things going on in my life then, Heather. Things I couldn't control."

"I know." Heather didn't like the way he was pacing across her room. "You hadn't recovered from your divorce. What had it been at that point? Six months since your wife had walked out? I thought that was long enough for you to have worked out your resentment, but it wasn't, was it? I read an article just the other day that says the anger can last a long time. Years even. It was my bad luck to get in your way before you'd finished punishing the female of the species for the actions of your ex-wife."

Flynn swung around, clearly annoyed at her analysis. "It wasn't just the divorce. There was a lot more to it than that."

"None of which I was responsible for," she reminded him quietly.

"I know that." Flynn came toward her with sudden deliberation, his eyes intent. "For heaven's sake, Heather, I've had eight months to realize what I did to you. Eight months to get everything back into perspective. I'm sorry, honey. I've never been sorrier about anything in my life than I am about the way I treated you. You loved me and I took your love and threw it back in your face. I was out of my head. But what happened is in the past. I'm back and this time things are going to be different. I guarantee it."

Heather flinched, stepping quickly out of reach as Flynn lifted his hand to touch the side of her face. For an instant panic assailed her, but almost immediately she got it under control.

"I don't know what kind of game you're playing, Flynn, but I don't want any part of it."

"I'm not playing any games." His hand fell back to his side and an unreadable emotion shadowed his eyes. "I'm here to take what you were offering eight months ago. This time I'll take good care of it and you, Heather."

She stared at him, dumbfounded. "You're serious, aren't you?"

"I've never been more serious in my life."

"You actually have the gall to show up on my doorstep after what you did to me and claim you want to start over? I know you probably don't have a great deal of respect for my intelligence, Flynn, but I can assure you I'm not *that* stupid."

"There was nothing stupid about what you did eight months ago," he told her softly. "You were a little naive, perhaps. A little reckless. Maybe a little unwary and much too soft for your own good, but you weren't stupid. Don't be afraid of me. This time around things are going to be different. I want you, Heather. I want us to have what we could have had before I went to Saudi Arabia if I hadn't been such a damn fool."

Heather shook her head in bemused disbelief. "I can't believe this. Either you fried your brains out in the sun, or you think I'm an idiot. Let me put this to you as simply as I can—I never want to see you again, Flynn Rammage. Why the hell do you think I quit my job at Con-Struct while you were out of the country? I don't want to be within a hundred yards of you. I want you out of my house and out of my life. Now."

"Heather, please listen to me—"

"I listened to you last time and look what it got me. I won't make the same mistake twice. I can only assume you were at loose ends tonight and decided you'd try for an easy roll in the sack with a woman who couldn't say no to you eight months ago. But you didn't understand the real reason I went to bed with you before you left Tucson. It wasn't because I couldn't say no. It was because I loved you. I no longer love you, Flynn. Therefore it's very easy to say no. Now get out of here before my guest arrives."

Flynn glanced at the open door and then pinned her beneath grim eyes. "I asked you once. Who is he?"

Heather smiled far too sweetly. "A friend who just recently went through a divorce. You know how that is. He needs a little warmth and comfort from a woman who *understands*."

Flynn's expression darkened into something quite dangerous, and then he appeared to take a firm grip on himself. He put out his hand again, ignoring Heather's automatic attempt at retreat. She was up against the wall and there was nowhere for her to run. Realizing it, she chose disdain over her instinctive urge to flee. When his rough-tipped fingers touched the side of her cheek she didn't move.

"I've missed you, Heather."

She forced a small, aloof smile. "You expect me to believe that?"

"I'm going to make you believe it." And then he was lowering his head, his warm, hungry mouth covering hers and silencing the protest behind her lips.

Heather's first reaction was astonishment. She should have been expecting the sensual attack, but for some reason she hadn't. Even as she recovered and began to struggle she knew she was doing the wrong thing. That was the problem with Flynn Rammage. She always did the wrong thing around him.

"Heather, honey, don't fight me. I've waited so long to hold you again." His voice was husky and persuasive. He cradled her head between his palms and took her mouth with an urgency that communicated itself to all of Heather's nerve endings.

She put her hands against his shoulders and shoved with all her might. It was like pushing against a rock wall. He didn't even seem to be aware of her resistance. Instead of reacting to it, Flynn simply folded her closer, stilling her hands by trapping them against his chest. His mouth continued to move on hers, his tongue sliding along her lower lip as he gently sought a way inside.

The easiest way out of this was passive resistance, Heather told herself wildly. She knew this man. There was a primitive, elemental side to him that was both passionate and dangerous. Fighting him would only excite his masculine urge to conquer her. Heart pounding, Heather forced herself to stand quietly.

He responded by deepening the kiss, parting her lips with his own and flicking his tongue hungrily into the moist warmth behind her teeth. Heather felt the intoxicating rush of hot memories, and closed her eyes fiercely against them. She would not be this man's victim again.

Flynn's hands slid down to Heather's waist and then went lower. He groaned and cupped her buttocks. "You can't have forgotten. I'll make you remember how it was between us." He lifted her up, forcing her into the heated cradle of his thighs.

Heather shivered as the excitement she thought she had forgotten after eight long months flooded her bloodstream anew. Only one man had ever had this impact on her senses, and she'd require all her self-control to resist it. But this time she *would* resist it, Heather promised herself fiercely. She wouldn't play the fool twice.

"Heather, honey, relax. It's going to be all right this time. I promise you, it's going to be all right." The words were heavy, heated honey. Flynn kept her pressed close to him, imprinting himself on every inch of her body. His mouth trailed hot, urgent kisses along her throat and then returned to her lips.

She wanted to scream, and simultaneously she wanted to surrender. Eight months ago she had fallen head over heels in love with this man, and all the walls she had erected against him since he had left were already showing fractures.

"Flynn, let me go. Please let me go. I don't want this. I don't want you. Can't you understand?"

"You're lying, sweetheart," he murmured. "I can feel the truth in you." He eased her back down so that she was again standing on the floor, and then crowded her close to the wall, his hands never releasing her. He let his fingertips slide upward until he could feel the curve of her breast. She gasped when he boldly grazed his thumbs over her nipples. The small intake of breath brought a glittering satisfaction to Flynn's eyes. "You want me," he whispered, and kissed her again.

"No," she declared, shoving at him with a suddenness that took both of them by surprise. "I won't let you do this to me. I'm not the idiotic fool I was eight months ago!"

Flynn stared broodingly down at her for a tense moment, as if he were waging an internal debate about how to handle her. Then slowly he released her and took a step backward. "I don't want to frighten you, Heather."

She moved away from him. "You're not frightening me—you're annoying me. Now that you've conducted your little experiment to see if I'd fall back into your hands like a ripe plum, will you please get out of here?"

"So that you can spend the night with the jerk who's recovering from his divorce?"

"So that I can spend the night doing whatever I want to do," she shot back. "And whatever that is, it's no business of yours, is it, Flynn?"

"Heather, you say you're not afraid of me."

"I'm not!"

"Will you have dinner with me tomorrow night?"

"No."

"Why not?"

"Because I don't want to waste an entire evening with you. I'm just moving in here, Flynn. This is the first home I've ever owned. It's what the real estate agents like to call a fixer-upper. As you can see there's a lot of fixing up to do. Frankly I'd rather clean the oven than go out to dinner with you. Does that give you a reasonably clear idea of how I feel on the subject of dating you?"

"We have a lot to talk about, honey. There are things I want to explain. Things I have to tell you."

"Unfortunately I don't have anything to say to you."

"You don't have to say a word." Flynn smiled faintly. "I'll do all the talking if that's the way you want it. But I don't think it will be a one-sided conversation for long. You and I could always talk, couldn't we, Heather? For hours."

Through the open door Heather saw a familiar red Ford slide into a parking space at the curb behind Flynn's Porsche. The car door opened and Lee Osborne got out. He reached inside and cautiously lifted a large, flat box off the front seat.

"You'll have to excuse me, Flynn," Heather said with mock formality. "My guest is here."

Flynn turned to glance back through the doorway at the good-looking redheaded man coming up the walk. "You never did tell me his name."

"Lee Osborne." Heather walked out the door and greeted the new arrival with a smile that held as much relief as it did welcome. "You're just in time. I was about to start on the wine without you. I'm famished."

"It took forever to get this damn pizza made up to your specifications," Lee complained good-naturedly. But his attention was on the silent man standing in the doorway behind Heather. "Anchovies and hot peppers aren't that popular a combination."

"Believe me, it will be worth the wait." Heather kept her smile at full brilliance as she added, "Lee, I want you to meet Flynn Rammage. He'd heard I've become a homeowner and stopped by to wish me good luck with the plumbing. I used to work for him at Con-Struct International before I saw the light and joined Talon and Associates. Flynn, this is Lee Osborne. He's an engineer at Talon."

The two men nodded with a minimum of politeness. What with Lee's hands full of pizza box and Flynn's reluctance to be civil it was easy to skip the formality of a handshake. Neither seemed to regret it.

"Osborne." Flynn glanced at Heather, his eyes coolly amused. "You didn't mention you'd gone to work for Con-Struct's chief local rival, Heather."

"You didn't ask." She hurried Lee up the stairs. "Flynn was just leaving, weren't you, Flynn?"

"Depends on how you look at it," Flynn said musingly as he came slowly down the steps. "Some might say I was just arriving."

"Yeah, well, nice to meet you, Rammage." Lee glanced back at the other man as Heather urged him into the hall.

Flynn halted on the walk and regarded the two in the doorway. His gaze skipped dismissingly over Osborne and settled on Heather's tensely smiling face. "Good night, Heather. I'll be seeing you soon. Remember that."

"I'm afraid I'm going to be awfully busy for quite a while," Heather informed him in a remarkably even tone. "Maybe I'll give you a call when I've got some free time," she added mockingly. Before Flynn could say anything further she slammed the front door and took the pizza box from Lee's hands. "Thank heavens you got here when you did. You know how it is with an old boss. You have to be polite, but they can be such bores. Come into the kitchen. The wine's been hyperventilating for hours."

"Just the way I like it," Lee assured her cheerfully.

As Heather set the pizza carton down on the counter she heard the low purr of Flynn's black-and-silver Porsche. As the sound of the car's engine receded into the distance she let out a long, silent sigh of relief.

Perhaps now the odd sensation of being watched that had bothered her all afternoon would disappear.

# Two

There was no doubt about it, Heather decided with blunt objectivity as she lay in bed that night. She had overreacted.

But it had been such a shock to open the door and find Flynn Rammage on the step. It was the last thing she had been expecting and she simply hadn't been prepared.

She turned on her side and pounded the pillow into a more comfortable shape. A scratching noise at the window caused her to start, until she realized it was just the sound of a tree branch sliding along the glass. This was the first night she had spent in her new house and there was going to be a variety of small sounds and squeaks she would have to grow accustomed to hearing in the evenings. Until now Heather had always lived in apartments, where the majority of odd sounds always came from the neighbors. It seemed strange not to have someone living on the other side of the bedroom wall, she thought. In an apartment one always had the comforting illusion that if one screamed one would be heard and something would be done about it. Living in a house was going to be a change.

But the change was going to be worth it. She gazed around the nearly empty room. A place of her own. She could still hardly believe it. Most of the rooms were empty at this point. She had always rented her furniture until now, telling herself she was saving for the good stuff while she saved for the down payment on the house. When she'd given up her apartment, she'd sent the rented furniture back to the rental agency. At the moment she was getting by on a narrow twin bed she had picked up dirt cheap at a yard sale and a card table with three folding chairs. There were a couple of stools in the kitchen that she had found at the same yard sale where she'd discovered the bed. Other than her stereo there wasn't much else in the house. She looked forward to shopping for real furniture. It was all part of the fun of creating her own home.

Her thoughts drifted back again to Flynn Rammage. Once more she allowed herself to relive the scene that had taken place in her living room earlier in the evening. She frowned as she went over it, trying to figure out a better way she could have handled it. Too bad she hadn't had some warning.

Lack of warning about Rammage had been the problem right from the beginning, however. Heather leaned back against the pillow, staring into the shadows, and thought about what she might have done differently eight months ago if someone had warned

her that Flynn Rammage was still recovering from a
messy divorce.

Unfortunately she had been very new at the firm of
Con-Struct International. She hadn't had time to
make close friends or become part of the office gos-
sip mill. Even if she had known, though, Heather told
herself with brutal honesty, she probably wouldn't
have behaved any differently. She would still have
found herself responding to the pain she had seen in
him.

That pain had been masked from most people by a
layer of sardonic masculine confidence that was second nature to Flynn. Heather decided that it was just
bad luck she had been so perceptive. For that matter,
Rammage had been pretty damn perceptive himself.
He had seen the compassion in her at once and he'd
zeroed in on it like a trained fighter pilot going in for
the kill.

She had been so vulnerable to him, Heather
thought, because she'd not only wanted to offer comfort to Flynn, she'd also wanted to offer herself. The
danger lay in the undeniable fact that Flynn had the
power to arouse not only her compassion, but also her
passion. It had been a lethal combination, one she'd
never dealt with in any other relationship.

Without any second thoughts, without an ounce of
caution, without any of her normal feminine wariness, Heather had opened herself to Flynn's deliberate overtures. Almost from the first he had talked,
really talked to her, rather than flirted with her. He
had known instinctively how to approach her, Heather
recalled. She might have erected a few of the normal
female defenses against him if he'd started his pursuit

with the usual masculine flirtation. But Flynn was far too wily a hunter for that.

The deliberate, meaningful conversations had quickly led to shared lunches and dinner dates that had led inevitably to bed. On one hand Heather had known that everything was happening much too fast, but on the other she had never experienced such an immediately intense relationship before in her life. This was different, she told herself. This was real. This man was unique. He was the one she had been waiting for and she could only thank her lucky stars that he seemed to feel the same way about her. He needed her and he wanted her. She willingly gave him everything she had to give.

The heated intensity of Flynn's lovemaking seemed to be an extension of the intensity of his whole approach to her. It was as if he had to have her, as if he'd been waiting forever for her. Even now Heather did not for a moment doubt his passion. That much had been real.

In a sense, she decided, his emotional need for her had been real, too. But Flynn had been too filled with rage, too desperate for someone to punish, to realize just why he was attracted to Heather.

He had told her very little about his ex-wife. Heather knew only that the woman had left Flynn to marry a professor at the University of Arizona, where she had been pursuing a master's degree. The ex-Mrs. Rammage and her new husband had moved to California a few months before Heather had taken the position at Con-Struct. Heather hadn't realized until too late that Flynn had not gotten over his raw fury. He had succeeded in concealing that from her. All she had seen was the underlying pain.

She still didn't know if his anger was based on the fact that he had loved his wife deeply, or if it was simply his reaction to what he deemed betrayal. Either way it had spelled doom for Heather.

The affair had been short-lived. Flynn had been interested only in Heather's surrender. She had given it wholeheartedly after only a few evenings spent lingering over conversation and brandy. She still remembered those evenings. Every word, every glance had seemed fraught with meaning. It was as if there had been two levels of communication, one verbal, one intangible, and they had both existed simultaneously. She had been sure Flynn had been reaching out to her, trying to establish a bond that was mental as well as physical.

Perhaps he had been, she told herself now. But if that was true, he hadn't been about to admit it to himself. He had taken her to bed every night for a couple of weeks, enveloping her in a sensual cloud that hadn't lifted until the morning when she had awakened to find him staring at her with an unreadable gaze. She could still feel a trace of the chill that she had experienced that morning when she'd looked into his tawny eyes and seen no future.

It was then he'd told her with a kind of grim casualness that he wouldn't be seeing her again. It had been fun, but it was over. He was leaving for Saudi Arabia in a few days. He didn't know how long he'd be gone. He might call her when he got back to the States. He said something about hoping she wasn't going to make things awkward at the office. Dazed, Heather had shaken her head, afraid that if she tried to say something she would end up crying. A short while later she'd managed to say goodbye far too po-

litely, and then she'd watched him walk out the door
of her apartment for the last time.

A week after that he'd left for Saudi Arabia. She
hadn't seen him again. The offices of Con-Struct International were large enough to ensure that acciden-
tal hallway meetings could be avoided. Heather had
her résumés in the mail before Flynn's plane had left
Tucson.

Heather pulled her mind back from the memories.
She had relived them too many times during the past
few months. For the most part they were under control now. She wanted to keep them that way.

It was only as she was finally drifting off to sleep
that Heather realized she still had the strange sensation of being watched. She had a brief, mental image
of Flynn prowling silently through the night, circling
her small fortress as he searched for a way inside, and
then she went to sleep.


Ten miles away Flynn sat in darkness, his feet
propped up on the slate coffee table, a glass of brandy
warming in his hands. It was late and he had been sitting there for quite a while, waiting for the brandy to
have some effect. It hadn't yet succeeded in blocking
the image of Heather sharing a pizza and a bottle of
cheap wine with a redheaded engineer named Lee Osborne. What really bothered him was wondering
whether Heather and Osborne would go on to share a
bed after the pizza and wine.

Flynn contemplated the shadows around him and
reminded himself that he was hardly in a position to
complain about how Heather chose to spend her evenings. He'd been a bastard eight months ago and she

seemed to agree. He'd been praying that she wouldn't concur so completely with that conclusion.

*Face it, Rammage,* he thought, *you were hoping you could walk back in on her and pick up right where you left off. You knew it wasn't going to be that easy.* But he'd been so sure that he'd at least get a hearing this evening. Instead he'd been kicked out while the door was being held open for another man.

Another *divorced* man. Rammage scowled and tried another swallow of brandy. Maybe Heather was specializing in helping males recover from their divorces. His fingers tightened fiercely around the snifter.

The sudden sound of crying brought him out of his moody reverie. Flynn was on his feet almost at once, setting the brandy glass down on the table in front of him. He strode quickly down the hall to the bedroom at the far end and pushed open the door. The crying became a sobbing wail. Flynn walked into the room.

"Hey, kid," he said softly to the small form huddled in the middle of the bed. "It's okay. I'm here. What's the problem?"

His soon-to-be four-year-old son clutched a ragged scrap of an old blanket and wailed all the more loudly. Jeremy Rammage put out his arms in a demanding plea and Flynn reached down to scoop him up.

"Bad dreams?" Flynn said soothingly. "What do four-year-olds dream about, I wonder. It's okay, son. It's okay." He patted Jeremy a little awkwardly, but the boy didn't seem to mind Flynn's approach. He began to quieten almost immediately, although he kept a firm grip on his father and the scraggly piece of blanket.

"So," Flynn said conversationally as the sobbing ceased, "what's up?"

"It was dark," Jeremy informed him, peering intently into Flynn's face to see if his father understood the significance of that.

"It does tend to get dark at night." Flynn smiled. "Want to join me for a nightcap out in the living room? Sometimes it takes the edge off the darkness."

Jeremy didn't quite understand the question, but he nodded a quick affirmative. Flynn carried his son in one strong arm as he walked back down the hall. In the gleaming modern kitchen Flynn settled Jeremy into a chair and then rummaged through the assortment of French cookware, food processors, coffee grinders and the latest in gourmet gadgetry until he found a plastic cup. Opening the two-door chrome-finished refrigerator he found a carton of milk. Carefully he poured the liquid into the cup and handed the drink to Jeremy, who took it eagerly.

"Okay, kid, let's go have a man-to-man talk. I could use a little advice from a slick operator such as you." Flynn headed for the living room and Jeremy ambled along behind him, dragging the blanket scrap and slurping happily on his cup of milk.

When Flynn sat back down on the gold leather couch and repropped his booted feet on the slate table Jeremy scrambled up into his father's lap.

"What do you think, kid?"

"Dark," Jeremy informed him in a positive tone.

"I know. Sometimes it's easier to think in the dark. And I've got a lot of thinking to do. Your old man struck out today. Did you know that? I really blew it. This is going to be tougher than I originally thought. She's got all the defenses in place now that she should have had eight months ago."

Flynn reached for his brandy glass and he and his son sipped their nightcaps in companionable silence for a while. "It occurs to me," Flynn finally went on after a time, "that you may be my ace in the hole. She doesn't know about you, kid. I never told her about you." Flynn broke off abruptly, remembering why he hadn't mentioned his son to Heather. "If I don't make any headway on my own maybe I'll let you take a shot at softening her up. What do you think?"

"It's still dark." Jeremy sounded a little sleepy now, but basically willing to oblige his father.

"She's really not very hard," Flynn assured the boy. "Soft as wildflowers and warm as sunshine. She came to me so easily the first time. I didn't even know what I had in my hands. And she felt so good in my hands. This time around things will be different. But first I've got to convince her of that. I think she still wants me, kid. I could feel the want in her this evening when I kissed her. Does that sound egotistical? Well, what the hell. It's just us men talking. I sure want her. Tell you what. I'll try getting her back on my own, and if I decide I'm botching the job I'll bring on the heavy artillery—you."

"Don't like the dark," Jeremy mumbled, half-asleep. The cup began to slide from his grasp.

Flynn caught the cup and gently removed it from Jeremy's fingers. "I'll leave the night-light on," he promised the boy softly as he got to his feet and carried him back to his room. "Maybe I ought to leave one on for myself. It gets lonely at night."

The ladder was old, and it wobbled slightly as Heather braced herself on the top step and began to screw a light bulb into one of the fixtures in the new track lighting system she'd had installed that afternoon. The doorbell chimed halfway through the task.

Pleased that the electrician who had installed the lighting had also gotten the doorbell working, she yelled "Come in," and continued twisting the bulb into the socket.

The door opened to reveal a mass of dazzling yellow chrysanthemums. "What the devil are you doing on that ladder? It looks like it's going to collapse at any moment."

Heather glanced at the boots beneath the huge collection of yellow flowers. Grimly she continued twisting the light bulb. "Hello, Flynn. What are you going to do with the flowers? Open a florist shop?"

"They're for you. Where do you want them?"

Heather finished her task and took a couple of steps down the shaky ladder. She folded her arms on the top perch and leaned on them as she studied Flynn. His tawny eyes met hers through a spray of yellow. "Why?"

"Why what? Why the flowers? Because I wanted to bring them."

"Why?" she repeated patiently.

"You used to love yellow chrysanthemums. Are you going to question everything I say or do?"

She considered that. "Yes, I think so. It's safer that way."

"If you were really safety conscious you wouldn't be standing on that ladder. Did you have the wiring in the place checked out? I'll bet it's a disaster. Get down and we'll discuss the matter of where you want these flowers." He started toward the kitchen without waiting for an invitation or directions.

Heather came slowly down off the ladder, dusting her hands on her jeans, and followed Flynn into the kitchen. He was in the process of putting the bundle of chrysanthemums into the sink. When he started to turn on the faucet Heather finally capitulated. "I've got some glass jars you can use as vases."

He looked up, one eyebrow crooking wryly. "Your gracious acceptance of my humble offering overwhelms me."

Heather set her teeth as she opened a cupboard and took down two empty mayonnaise jars. "What did you expect, Flynn? That I'd throw myself at your feet the moment you reappeared on my doorstep?"

He grinned faintly and leaned casually against the counter while she arranged the flowers. "I'll admit that in a few of my wildest dreams I did run that scenario once or twice, but in my more rational moments I tried to be realistic. I knew this wasn't going to be easy. Have dinner with me tonight, Heather."

She frowned intently as she worked with the flowers. "Sorry, I've got too much to do around here, and besides, I don't feel like going to the trouble of changing clothes."

"We'll go someplace where you won't have to worry about your clothes. There's a taco joint a few blocks from here. You're dressed perfectly for it. Afterward I'll give you a hand putting in the rest of those light bulbs. Please come with me, Heather. I just want to talk to you."

Her hands stilled on the flowers as Heather frantically tried to decide what to do next. She'd never heard Flynn Rammage ask for anything in such a humble tone before. She wasn't sure she liked him in this role.

It would be much easier to keep him at a distance if he kept to his old, arrogant ways.

"Flynn, I think it would be a waste of everyone's time, including your own."

"I can guarantee it won't be a waste of my time."

Heather finished stuffing the last chrysanthemum stem into the jar and turned to face him. "I'm telling you right now that I won't climb back into bed with you," she said quietly.

He hesitated, his gaze serious. "All I'm asking for tonight is dinner and some of your time."

"You want something more than that, Flynn. I'm not entirely without brains."

"I want to talk to you. I'm not asking you to go to bed with me."

She looked away, uneasy under that intent gaze. The mass of yellow flowers held her full attention. Flynn had been right. She loved yellow chrysanthemums.

There were two ways of handling Flynn Rammage that were probably both guaranteed to fail. One was to surrender without a fight, as she had the first time around. The second was to run from him as if he were a demon hunter from Hades. The first method was obviously not a very intelligent approach. She'd already proved that much. Instinct warned her that the second method was dangerous because Rammage would react to the challenge with all-out pursuit. Heather had a horrible suspicion that in that race she was sure to lose.

The only other method she could think of at the moment was casual, disinterested civility. Besides, she was hungry.

She smiled coolly. "All right, Flynn, I'll let you buy me dinner. I guess you owe me that much, don't you?"

He didn't return the smile. "I owe you a lot more than that. Going to collect?"

"Are you offering me a little revenge?"

He shrugged. "Why not? You deserve it."

She shook her head ruefully. "Too late. If you'd come around with that offer six or seven months ago, I'd probably have taken you up on it. Unfortunately I'm over that stage now."

"I doubt if you would have been very successful at it six or seven months ago," Flynn said with a strange gentleness. He ran his finger lightly along her lower lip. "You're too soft for revenge, sweetheart. You'd wind up feeling sorry for your victim and that would be the end of the whole scheme."

Heather tried not to feel the leashed sensuality in his touch. She refused to flinch from it. "I think you underrate the inner fortitude of the female of the species, Flynn."

"Going to teach me a lesson on the subject?"

"It's time someone did."

"Let's go have a taco and a beer and discuss the matter," he challenged softly.

Heather didn't know whether to laugh or cry over the male anticipation she saw in his eyes. Flynn Rammage might claim he was feeling penitent and humble, but the truth was, he was as bold about taking what he wanted as ever. But this time around she was wise to him, Heather told herself. She could handle him.

"The taco and beer sound good," she admitted. "But let's skip the postmortems and meaningful discussions, okay? I'm not in the mood."

"Whatever you want, Heather."

She didn't believe that for a moment, but she went to find her shoulder bag, anyway.

The black-and-silver Porsche was as unabashedly sexy as she had remembered. She knew Flynn loved the car with the kind of enthusiasm only men seemed able to develop for automobiles. The barely civilized growl of the engine, the scent of leather and the close confines of the cockpit all combined to renew old memories Heather would rather have forgotten. She tried to put them from her as Flynn guided the Porsche away from the curb and out onto a busier thoroughfare.

"When did you decide to buy the house?" he asked, downshifting for a light with easy skill.

"I've been saving for a home of my own for a long time."

"You never mentioned it when we..." He didn't finish the sentence.

"No, I didn't. We had a lot of deep conversations a few months ago, but there were several things we failed to discuss, weren't there?"

"Such as the future?" he suggested deliberately.

"That was definitely one of them," she agreed with a bland indifference she realized she was far from feeling. "But given the fact that there wasn't any future for us, it would have been a pointless conversation."

Flynn's hand tightened briefly on the wheel, and then he deliberately relaxed his grip. "The future is one of the things I'd like to talk about tonight."

"Forget it."

"All right, we'll start with the past," he announced with a touch of familiar assertiveness. "There are some things I want to explain to you, honey. I'm not going to try to justify the way I behaved eight months ago, but I want you to know exactly what was going on at the time. I want you to know why I was so angry at the world and every woman in it."

"I know why you were angry. You were still getting over your divorce. And you're absolutely right—it doesn't justify your actions. Nothing would."

Flynn scowled at the taillights of the car ahead of him. "It wasn't the divorce, exactly. Cheryl and I had been having problems for quite a while. She wanted out of the marriage and I knew it. By the time she finally filed for divorce, I didn't care much one way or the other about her, but there were other factors involved."

"I don't want to hear about them," Heather said firmly.

He ignored her, continuing his explanation with dogged persistence. "At the time I met you, I had just been through a disaster of a court action that had left me—"

"If you're going to tell me it left you broke, forget it. Every man who goes through divorce in this country claims he got taken to the cleaners. But the truth is, studies have shown that after a divorce women are thrown into a much lower economic bracket, while the man's financial situation improves considerably. So don't give me any sob stories about what the divorce cost you. This car alone would make a liar out of you."

"You seem to have become quite an expert on divorce since I last saw you," Flynn muttered grimly.

"Ummm. I've discovered it's a necessity for a single woman of my age," Heather agreed quite brightly. "After a woman turns thirty she makes the rather horrifying discovery that all the good men in her age group are married or gay. It seems like the only available males left are either married and looking for an affair, or divorced and looking for an affair. It's a tough world out there for the single woman in her thirties these days."

"I see. The fact that you're involved with Lee Osborne means you've opted to stick with the divorced crowd?"

Heather heard the rough, possessive jealousy behind the words and wondered at it. "Lee and I are just friends," she found herself saying almost placatingly. It irritated her that she even bothered to try to soothe him. She owed Flynn exactly nothing, Heather reminded herself.

"What kind of a future is Osborne offering? What exactly does *friendship* entail these days?"

"Not much," Heather said, deliberately keeping her words as light as possible. She didn't like the dark intensity that was creeping into the conversation.

"I'm offering a hell of a lot more than friendship, Heather. And I'm also offering more than an affair."

"Please, Flynn. You're ruining my appetite. Look, is that the taco joint you had in mind?"

He glared at the neon sign looming up on the right-hand side of the street. "Yeah, that's it. But, Heather, I'm trying to explain something to you. Will you please listen?"

"No. I figure that may have been my major problem eight months ago. I did too much listening. You always had a way with words. There's a parking space over there to the left of the entrance."

"I see it," Flynn growled.

The small restaurant was crowded and noisy. Flynn had obviously not expected either the people or the loud chatter going on around the small table where he and Heather were seated. They had to raise their voices in order to give the waitress their orders for tacos, tamales and two bottles of Mexican beer. When the beer and two glasses arrived Flynn took a long swallow and leaned forward in an effort to make himself heard.

"Why Talon and Associates?"

"What?" Heather leaned back in her chair, more or less defeating Flynn's attempt to create a measure of conversational intimacy. She savored her beer and waited for him to repeat the question. It bought her a few seconds in which to analyze it.

"You heard me. I said, why did you go to Talon and Associates?" Flynn's expression was hooded as he sat leaning forward with his big hands wrapped around the glass. "You must have known they're Con-Struct's major rivals in town."

"The fact didn't escape me," Heather admitted with a small smile.

Flynn's expression darkened further. "Take anything useful with you?"

Heather was grinning now. "It would have been easy, wouldn't it? People tend to forget just how much company proprietary information the manager of a central filing operation has access to in the course of her work. Con-Struct's filing system is all computerized and I was in charge of search and retrieval on the computers. Yes, indeed. It would have been a snap to take all sorts of interesting documents with me.''

"Did you?"

Heather's grin faded. She took another swallow of her beer. ''What do you think?''

Flynn studied her for a long moment and then sat back slowly in his chair. Heather almost didn't hear him when he finally spoke. ''I don't think you bought your way into the Talon job with any Con-Struct proprietary materials. You're not the type.''

Oddly enough his unexpected faith in her professional integrity warmed Heather. The feeling lasted for all of ten seconds before she reminded herself that maybe she shouldn't be flattered. It probably only meant that Flynn didn't think she had the guts or the resolve to take such a drastic revenge.

Heather didn't respond to his declaration. She told herself she was under absolutely no obligation to carry the burden of conversation. Eight months ago she had felt differently. The deep, purposeful conversations with Flynn had been enormously important to her. They had seemed a bright omen of the future, a sure indication that she could really communicate with this man and an assurance that he wanted to communicate on a meaningful level with her. That was before she had learned that such conversations were merely a tool of seduction that Flynn wielded particularly well.

Across the table Flynn watched Heather moodily. When she continued to sit quietly, drinking her beer and gazing around the room with mild interest, he sighed heavily and leaned forward once more in an attempt to force some intimacy.

"Heather, I know you don't want to listen to me tonight, but there are some things that have to be said."

"Not now, Flynn. Here comes the food." She eyed the brimming platters of tacos and tamales with the first genuine enthusiasm she had exhibited that evening.

Flynn waited impatiently while the food was set down in front of them. When the waitress had bustled off he tried again to make himself heard above the cheerful din. "Damn it, Heather, this is important. I have something to say to you, and you, by God, are going to listen."

"Can you speak up, Flynn? It's so noisy in here." Heather splashed hot sauce on her taco and took a giant, crunchy bite.

Quite suddenly the room went silent in the way that a crowded room sometimes does. Unfortunately for Flynn there was no warning and his next words were already half out of his mouth. They fell loudly into the unexpected lull, audible in every corner of the restaurant. Everyone's head turned.

"Damn it to hell, Heather, will you please pay attention? I'm asking you to marry me!"

# Three

Heather was still having trouble controlling her laughter when Flynn finally stuffed her unceremoniously back into the Porsche and slid in beside her.

"I'm glad you find the whole thing so amusing," he muttered as he turned the key savagely in the ignition.

"I do." Heather struggled to contain another fit of giggles. "To tell you the truth, it was the funniest thing I've experienced in weeks. It made me realize how little laughing we did together eight months ago. Lots of heavy conversation but very little laughter." It was true, she realized suddenly. She hadn't thought about it until tonight, but she suddenly realized that humor had been an ingredient that had been distinctly absent in her relationship with Flynn.

"In case it escaped your notice, I was definitely not laughing tonight." He shoved the car into gear with a controlled violence that sent the Porsche racing onto the street.

"Too bad. Everyone else in the restaurant was."

"Including you."

"Maybe someday when you're ninety-five or so you'll look back and see the humor of the situation."

"I doubt it." There was a tense silence for a few moments and then Flynn went on aggressively. "In any event, I didn't get an answer."

Heather's laughter finally faded. "No, you didn't, did you? That was partially because I was too busy watching you recover from the scene you had created. And partially because I couldn't believe what I was hearing."

"I meant it, Heather," he assured her quietly. "I want you to marry me."

"Why?"

"For God's sake, will you stop questioning everything I say or do? I want you to marry me for the usual reasons, damn it."

"What are your usual reasons, Flynn?" she asked with deep interest.

He shot her a sidelong glance, clearly trying to assess her mood before he committed himself. "Has it occurred to you that I'm in love with you?"

"No." She waited expectantly.

He scowled, his hand on the gearshift again as he slowed for a red light. "You don't believe me?"

"No," she repeated. "But I'll admit I am getting curious. What's going on here, Flynn?"

"Eight months of wanting you is what's going on, damn it. Can't you understand that? I didn't have to take that Saudi Arabian job, you know. I could have stayed here and sent someone else to manage the project. I grabbed that job for myself because I knew I had to get away for a while. I needed time to think. Time to work things out. Things that had been eating me alive before I left Tucson. You said earlier you didn't want to hear about them, but I want to explain. You always understood things, Heather. You were always *willing* to understand them."

"Did your private problems justify the way you treated me?"

Flynn swore softly as he eased the Porsche into a parking space in front of Heather's home. "I've already told you they didn't. I'm not trying to make excuses. I'm trying to get you to understand."

"I'm not in the understanding business anymore." Heather opened her car door without waiting for him. "Thanks for the meal and the proposal, Flynn. You certainly livened up an otherwise dull evening."

He slammed out of the car and strode up the walk behind her, reaching the door before she could close it in his face. Without any apology he shoved his foot over the threshold and eased himself into the hall. "Heather, I've asked you to marry me," he said steadily. "The question deserves a polite, considered response. Whatever you may think of me, you know I've never lied to you. I'm offering marriage and it's an honest offer. I want an honest answer, not some flippant attempt to put me in my place."

Heather felt her mouth go dry as she looked up at him. He was serious and she knew it. The knowledge shot through her senses, making her pulse beat faster and threatening whatever control she had over her responses. Eight months ago she had loved this man with a willing, eager heart. Some things, she was discovering, don't change.

"I don't know why you're doing this to me, Flynn. I can't believe you're so desperate to get me back into bed that you would lie about marriage."

He moved before she could retreat, taking her in his arms and folding her close. "It's not a lie," he muttered thickly. "I want you and I want marriage. What's more, I think you still want me, too. In spite of everything I did to you. Believe me, Heather, when I tell you that eight months ago I was so involved with my own anger that I didn't realize what I was throwing aside when I let you go. I've had time to think."

Heather stood perfectly still, her eyes wide and luminous as she looked up at him. Very deliberately she repeated what she had said earlier that evening. "I will not go to bed with you, Flynn."

"I'm not asking you to go to bed with me. Not tonight. Please, Heather, kiss me. Kiss me just once the way you used to before I behaved like a fool and put an end to everything."

It was the aching need she saw in him that overrode Heather's common sense. In the past she had been so terribly susceptible to that need, and that was something else that apparently hadn't changed. Instinctively she found herself responding. Her hands had been braced against his shoulders and now her nails sank into the fabric of his shirt in a silent display of her inner reaction. Flynn felt the gentle kneading touch and groaned. His mouth came down on hers.

Heather whispered his name and then she could say nothing else. His lips were warm and compelling on hers, but there was no arrogance or demand in the kiss. It was a tender, sensual caress that was clearly under restraint. Flynn wasn't going to push her. Sensing that, Heather allowed herself to respond.

Her arms stole around his neck and her body leaned into the warmth and strength of his. She could feel the heat and need in him just as she had been able to feel it all those months ago. It reached out to pull her into the ancient masculine trap, and Heather knew she was getting entangled in the shimmering web. *But this much had been real,* she thought. The passion had been honest.

"Heather, honey, it's going to be all right this time. I swear it." Flynn's words were a ragged promise that he repeated over and over again as he sank down onto the carpet. He pulled her with him, settling her across his legs so that she was cradled against his chest.

Heather's senses began to spin as Flynn deepened the kiss. His hand stroked along her shoulder and down her arm as he thrust the tip of his tongue between her lips. Heather kept her eyes closed, holding old memories at bay but unable to stop new ones from taking shape. She heard the soft, sexy little moan, and belatedly realized she was the one who had made the small sound. Her arms crept more tightly around Flynn's neck.

He pulled her closer. Beneath her thigh she could feel the undeniable hardness of him. His fingers slipped off her arm and onto her hip. He touched her as if the very shape of her were something he had been craving for a long while. His palm curved around her thigh, fingers squeezing gently. There was no doubting the desire in him, but he handled her as if she were delicate crystal. The restraint he had placed on himself was as obvious as it was unexpected.

Heather marveled at the tenderness of his caresses. Flynn's lovemaking had always been excitingly passionate, his approach bold and sensual, but she didn't remember this element of aching tenderness. It was new and it was unbelievably seductive. She had been prepared to withstand the whirlwind, and found herself dealing, instead, with a soft evening breeze. How did one fight the softest of breezes, the kind that brought the clean, warm, spicy scent of the desert with them? She had always loved the desert. Perhaps she had been fated to always love this man.

"You don't know how I've missed the feel of you, sweetheart." Flynn breathed the words against her throat as he tasted her in a series of clinging little kisses that brought another sigh from Heather. Her arms tightened around him and she nestled closer to the waiting heat and hardness he offered. She let herself forget the past and the future, indulging her senses in the rich excitement they had learned months ago from Flynn. All the old need to give herself to him bubbled up inside her, as strong now as it had been eight months previously.

"Flynn," she murmured into his shirt. "It's been so long."

"I know," he whispered. "Believe me, I know." He flattened his hand on the curve of her stomach and moved it upward, skimming over her breasts. Then he slowly began to undo the buttons of the emerald green shirt she wore.

Heather could feel his fingers trembling slightly and she found the knowledge almost painfully endearing. Flynn was taking nothing for granted tonight, not even her surrender. His body was pleading with hers. He was not so much an aggressor as a supplicant. The knowledge gave Heather a sense of confidence. When he finished unfastening her shirt and moved his hand inside the fabric to cup her breast she realized she was hanging on to him as if for dear life. Her legs shifted restlessly as she turned her lips against the warm column of his throat.

"Ah, Heather, I've dreamed of this. You'll never know how often." Flynn groaned and cradled her closer. He gently caught one nipple between thumb and forefinger and urged it into full flower. Then he bent his head to kiss the throbbing peak. Heather shivered in his arms. "I won't hurt you," he muttered. "I swear I won't hurt you. Not this time."

She wasn't listening anymore. Her senses held full sway, responding completely now to the tender, stroking touches. As the fire of her inner excitement began to flame higher Heather became vaguely impatient. His gentleness had overcome her fears, but she was beginning to want more than the carefully restrained strokes and light, grazing touches she was receiving. She twisted a little in his hold, silently asking for more. It had been so long since she had felt like this. She remembered the storm and was ready to return to its center.

There was a faint rasping sound and Heather realized Flynn had undone the zipper of her jeans. With a fumbling movement she opened his shirt and slid her hand inside until she could feel his warm, smoothly muscled skin. The moment she wove her fingers eagerly into the crisp curling hair of his chest Heather felt Flynn's fingers glide into the soft nest above the juncture of her thighs. She moaned softly and lifted herself against his hand in gentle demand. Her nails bit slightly into his flesh.

*Now*, she thought wildly, *now you can let go and touch me the way you used to touch me.* She wanted to tell him there was no longer any need to hold himself in check. She was ready for the passionate storm of his lovemaking. She could feel the liquid heat in her body and knew he was already dampening his fingers in it.

But still Flynn's touch was light and cautious, far more delicate than she wanted at this point. Heather could feel the leashed power in him and knew he was burning with desire. She didn't understand how he could exert such self-control. He'd never bothered in the past. There had been no need to bother. She wanted to tell him there was no need to do so tonight, either, but the words were incoherent in her throat. Once more she strained against his hand. Then she nipped him lightly with her teeth.

In response Flynn lowered his head again and covered her mouth with his. Eagerly Heather pulled him closer, sure that now he would slip his own leash and take her with the compelling power he had always demonstrated in the past.

But he made no effort to change position or remove his clothes. Her jeans were down below her hips and Flynn finished sliding them off her legs. When she curled more tightly against him he slipped his tongue lightly into her mouth and slipped his hand just as lightly back under the silky edge of her panties.

Heather sucked in her breath and shuddered as she felt his fingertip glide over all the exquisitely sensitive areas hidden beneath. She clutched Flynn more tightly and even put one hand beseechingly on his arm in a silent effort to show him she was ready for the full strength of his passion.

What she got, instead, was a delicate, unbelievably tantalizing series of patterns traced over the secret area between her thighs. Heather thought she would go out of her mind. Flynn paid no attention to her silent pleas, continuing to tease her with the lightest of touches until she was a shivering bundle of femininity in his arms.

Then he slipped his fingers inside her in a delicate, probing touch. Simultaneously he stroked his tongue deeply into her mouth.

All the mounting tension within Heather exploded. The fire went to flashpoint and she cried out her satisfaction in a soft, breathless voice that was lost beneath Flynn's mouth.

He held her tightly while the convulsions gripped her, wrapping her close as she whispered his name over and over again. Then, slowly, languorously, she quieted against him, and reality settled back into place.

"I want you, Heather. More than I've ever wanted anything in my life," Flynn said into her tousled hair as he held her to him.

She blinked, bemused by the aftereffects of the passion he had induced. Her senses were no longer spinning and she was beginning to think clearly again. She knew Flynn's arousal was still at an unsatisfied peak. She could feel the straining tautness beneath the denim of his jeans, was fully aware of the expectant hardness in his muscles. The heat in him was still so intense it should have scorched her. But he made no move to lay her down on the carpet and cover her body with his own.

"All right?" he whispered.

She nodded, aware that she should be the one asking the question. He was obviously in the grip of a fierce, unsatisfied need. She wondered why he didn't try to do something about it. Then it finally occurred to Heather that Flynn Rammage was waiting for an engraved invitation from her.

She sat up slowly, looking at him through the veil of her lashes. He was watching her with silent hunger. The first licking flames of uncertainty came to life within her. *She should never have let things go this far.*

Flynn watched as the expressions of doubt and regret chased themselves through her shadowed hazel eyes and he exhaled heavily. Then a wry curve edged his mouth. He glanced at the black metal watch on his wrist.

"I think I'd better be on my way. It's getting late."

Startled, Heather automatically glanced at her own watch. It wasn't even nine-thirty. Flynn had certainly never excused himself on such flimsy grounds before. But she wasn't about to argue with him. She was feeling guilty enough as it was for having let him pleasure her so completely while giving him nothing in return.

It didn't help her conscience much to tell herself he undoubtedly deserved it. She wasn't a tease and she didn't like being cast in the role of one, even if what had happened had not been entirely her fault. But she was too wary of him to offer the engraved invitation he'd apparently wanted. Something within her refused to make it that easy for him.

Awkwardly Heather struggled to her feet, reaching for her jeans and tugging them on quickly. Flynn uncoiled beside her, his hand under her arm. He rested his hands on her shoulders and kissed her forehead lightly. His tawny eyes glittered as he looked down at her for a long moment.

"Good night, Heather."

"Good night, Flynn." She couldn't think of anything else intelligent to say, so she added lamely, "Drive carefully."

He nodded. "I will. Think about my proposal, hmmm?"

It was probably all she was going to be able to think about, Heather thought, but aloud she said lightly, "Are you sure you want me to think about it? I might say yes. Then where would you be?"

He grinned. "Climbing into bed with you, instead of going home to a cold shower."

Something tightened within her. She didn't understand him and that made her wary. It wasn't in Flynn's nature to go through such an elaborate seduction scene without demanding his own satisfaction. At least it hadn't been in the nature of the Flynn Rammage she had known eight months ago. His obvious restraint tonight didn't fit into what she knew of this man.

"Good night, Flynn," she said again.

He nodded once, his brief amusement fading back into the more familiar brooding watchfulness. Then he walked toward the door, opened it and disappeared into the night without a backward glance.

Heather stood staring at the closed door for a long while, listening to the roar of the Porsche as it trailed into the distance. Confusion and caution swamped her.

She could not make sense of his actions tonight. That fact was both alarming and provoking. It was also dangerously intriguing.

Heather finally moved, wandering slowly through the house, turning off lights. Over and over again she asked herself the most unanswerable question of all.

Why marriage?

Why, after all this time and after the way he had left her eight months ago, was Flynn Rammage back on her doorstep, asking her to marry him? Heather was almost afraid to allow herself to examine the possibility that he had actually come to the conclusion he loved her. When the thought flicked across her mind she deliberately tried to squash it. She mustn't let herself build false hopes.

But the passion had been very real eight months ago. Perhaps now that his anger toward his ex-wife had receded and he was no longer consumed with a need to punish the entire female sex, Flynn had begun to realize just what he could have had with Heather.

Heather walked into the kitchen, flicked off a light and headed for the guest room. She was playing with fire when she allowed herself to imagine that Flynn had come to his senses and acknowledged his need of her. She knew it, but she couldn't avoid the shimmering hope that thought brought to life within her.

Once more she thought about the unselfish way he had made love to her tonight. Eight months ago Flynn would never have behaved in such a manner. He would have ensured her satisfaction, but he would also have made damn sure of his own.

*He wouldn't have waited politely for an invitation.* Nor, when one was not immediately forthcoming, would he have gently bade her good-night and exited without further reproach.

Heather winced as she stepped into the guest bedroom. One thing was for certain. Flynn had succeeded in thoroughly confusing her. He had also managed to restoke the embers of a fire she had hoped was extinguished. Worst of all, he'd made her start thinking again of a future that included him.

She was contemplating that dangerous dream, when she noticed that the door of the walk-in closet was ajar. Her brows came together consideringly as she tried to recall if she had closed it that morning after she had run the vacuum over the carpet inside.

Curiously she opened the door farther and switched on the light inside the closet. There were two distinct footprints marring the neatly vacuumed carpet. The prints were definitely not her own. They could only have been made by a man's shoes.

Thoughtfully Heather turned off the light and closed the door. The electrician must have wandered into the closet earlier in the day while he checked for wiring problems. It was the only logical explanation.

Slowly Heather moved into her bedroom and began to undress. Her mind filled with half-formulated hopes that she couldn't banish, she brushed her teeth and climbed into the narrow single bed.

Her last memories before she fell asleep concerned an offer of marriage and the elusive hope that perhaps, after all this time, Flynn Rammage had realized he had fallen in love with her.

Three days later Heather was as confused as ever, but the hope within her had grown steadily. It had continued to flower because Flynn had been careful to do everything he could to nourish it—Heather wasn't so besotted that she didn't realize that. But the fact that he was making such an effort only captivated her all the more. She was coming to the conclusion that he was genuinely serious about marriage. Flynn had shown up on her doorstep every evening since that scene in the Mexican restaurant. He arrived with flowers and sometimes food. He never stayed late, and he hadn't repeated the lovemaking. He seemed content now to touch her with casual intimacy and kiss her lightly when he said good-night. Heather didn't know what to make of the whole thing.

Flynn had reminded her once that he had never lied to her, and Heather had to admit that much was the truth. The first time around she had foolishly fed herself on rainbows and dreams, but Flynn had never talked of a future or of his feelings for her other than those that involved physical passion.

The serious, intent conversations that had seduced Heather so easily had revolved around philosophies of life, the latest headlines from the Middle East and the future of Con-Struct International. Flynn had talked to her of his plans for the future of the firm, but not of his plans for his own future. She had seen the pain that still lingered in his eyes and had thought it was too early for such discussions. She had been willing to wait, offering solace and love in the meantime, convinced that the powerful passion they shared had its roots in an emotional and intellectual bond.

She had been devastated by the abrupt way he had broken off the relationship. But even when she had begun to understand how she had been used to assuage his fury at the female of the species, Heather had to admit he had never actually lied to her. He had simply allowed her to delude herself. And she had done so with a brilliant flourish.

"Hey, Heather, it's Friday. What are you doing working so hard? Want to have lunch with Terry and me?"

Heather looked up from her desk and smiled at the woman in the doorway. Beth Montgomery was in her early thirties, an attractive dark-haired woman who was divorced and raising two kids alone. She worked in the planning office of Talon and Associates.

"Actually," Heather said, "that's the best idea I've heard all day. I haven't got the faintest idea why I'm working so hard on a Friday. I don't know what got into me. Where's Terry?"

"She's on her way." Beth glanced over her shoulder. "Coming down the hall now. She had to finish up a report for Nevins."

Heather got to her feet, retrieved her shoulder bag from a bottom desk drawer and stepped out into the hall to greet Terry Kent. Terry had just turned thirty-one and had never been married. She was a pleasingly plump woman with laughing blue eyes and a flair for clothes that made her a striking sight in the halls of Talon and Associates. Heather had gotten to know both Terry and Beth shortly after taking the job at Talon. During the past few months the three women had become friends. Lunch together had become a familiar routine.

"Jeez, what a day," Terry complained breezily as the three women seated themselves around a table at a nearby café. "Nevins has been a bear all morning. Had to have that stupid report out by noon, even though he won't be able to distribute it until Monday. Lucky for him I'm in such a cheerful mood today." She looked at her friends expectantly.

Heather grinned. "I'll bite. Why are you in such a cheerful mood today?"

"She's got a date tonight," Beth explained with a chuckle. "Lee Osborne from accounting. You know him, don't you?"

Heather nodded and then added quickly. "We're just friends."

"I," announced Terry, "intend to get beyond mere friendship with the man." She glanced at Heather with sudden concern. "Any objections?"

"Nope," Heather assured her. "He's all yours. I've been out with Lee a couple of times and he's very nice, but all he talks about is his divorce."

"Another divorced man." Beth groaned.

"What available man in our age bracket isn't? It's either date the divorced ones or start looking seriously at the twenty-year-olds, and frankly, it's hard to get excited about a child."

"Some men manage to stay infantile all their lives." Beth sighed. "Take my ex-husband for example. Never did grow up."

"I don't think Lee has that problem," Heather said reassuringly to Terry. "He's just floundering a little as he adjusts to being single again. He really is quite nice. He and I just didn't click. We're destined to remain friends."

"Good," said Terry with relish. "In that case I'll feel free to pursue him in earnest. I think I'll have the superburger with the salad and French fries. I'll need my energy for tonight."

"I'll need some energy, too," Beth muttered. "Unfortunately not for a hot date. My son's got a football game after school. He'll be crushed if I'm not sitting in the stands."

"I take it his father doesn't go to the games?" Terry asked.

"Are you kidding? We haven't heard from his father since he found himself a beach bunny out in sunny California. I'm learning the joys and pitfalls of single parenthood," Beth said with a grimace. "Do you realize how long it's been since I've had a date?

There aren't many men out there who are eager to take on a ready-made family.''

Terry and Heather nodded in commiseration. Beth's trials were familiar ones to her friends. But Beth shook off her wry mood and grinned at Heather. "So what are you doing tonight while Terry's out seducing Osborne?"

Heather reflected on the phone call she'd had earlier from Flynn. "It looks like I have a date, too."

"No kidding." Terry pounced on the fact. "Who is he?"

"No one you know. He works at a different company. Con-Struct International. His name's Flynn Rammage."

"Rammage." Beth repeated the name thoughtfully. "Doesn't he own half of Con-Struct International? My boss is always talking about him. Con-Struct's a major rival of ours."

"Ummm." Heather decided on a salad.

"Another divorced male?" Terry inquired cheerfully.

Heather sighed. "Yup, I'm afraid so."

"More than just divorced," Beth said easily. "He's got a kid, too. I heard my boss mention it. A four-year-old. Rammage recently got custody, I think." She broke off as she saw the expression on Heather's face. "Didn't you know?"

Heather swallowed her feeling of amazement. "No, I had no idea. He never mentioned it."

"Well, just make sure you know what you're doing, Heather," Beth advised. "Rammage might just be looking for a good time, but if he mentions marriage, be careful. He's probably after a free housekeeper and baby-sitter to take over where his wife left off."

*If he mentions marriage, be careful.* Heather repeated the words to herself until she thought she would go crazy. And then a slow, burning anger flared to life within her.

Now at last she could make sense of Flynn's odd behavior. Everything fell into place with perfect logic. He was shopping around for a built-in baby-sitter and housekeeper—preferably one who was also reasonably interesting in bed. In other words, Flynn needed a wife. He hadn't needed or wanted one eight months ago, but things had changed, apparently. Now he had custody of a small boy. That made all the difference in the world.

# Four

Flynn was confused and he didn't like the sensation. It was an unfamiliar one and it made him uneasy. He sat across the table from Heather and tried to make sense of her too bright mood.

Everything about Heather was a little too bright tonight. She was dressed in a scarlet dinner dress that hugged her curves in no uncertain terms. A provocative flounce of red feathers filled in the extravagantly cut neckline. The hemline was short, revealing a great deal of leg that ended in tiny red high heels. She wore a flashy ring, the stones so huge and glittery that it was obvious at a glance they were bold fakes. The clip that held her hair in its casual twist was equally bright. Flynn had never seen her dressed quite like this, and he'd been rather taken back when she'd answered the door earlier this evening. It had taken severe self-restraint not to comment on the racy outfit. After the marriage, he promised himself, he would exercise a little more influence over Heather's wardrobe. It was one thing for her to tease him in private. It was quite another for his wife to wear this sort of thing in public. Besides, it was hardly Heather's style, which only confused him further.

Her manner tonight was as bright and flashy as her clothing. More than once this evening she had flirted with him outrageously. Whenever he tried to pursue a serious discussion she changed the topic. She chatted cheerfully about everything from the weather to his experiences in the Middle East, but she wouldn't let any of the discussions become involved. She flitted from one topic to another like a scarlet butterfly darting from flower to flower. Flynn was not only confused, he was getting a little irritated. That last was not a welcome sign. He had promised himself he would be the perfect gentleman around Heather, with the emphasis on gentle.

Until tonight she had been full of caution and uncertainty. He'd caught glimpses of the banked embers of love in her eyes and three nights ago he had been unable to resist rekindling the passion in her. He'd tortured himself with memories of that sweet, feminine excitement for eight long months. It had taken all his self-control to walk out the door that night. Flynn had sensed that with only a small push he could have had everything he wanted in the way of physical satisfaction. But he'd been determined not to push her into anything. He wanted Heather to trust him sufficiently to freely invite him into her bed.

So, what, he asked himself aggrievedly, had happened to his sweet, cautious, uncertain Heather, the lady with the wealth of half-concealed, aching long-ing in her eyes?

"Had the most fascinating conversation at lunch today with some friends of mine," Heather was say-ing breezily as the watercress and romaine salad was placed in front of her by a skillful waiter. "All about the perils of dating these days."

Flynn scowled, sensing danger. "You, I assume, contributed your share to the conversation?"

"Not really. I just listened and learned." Heather smiled. Her lipstick was Ferrari red. "One of my friends who's raising two kids mentioned how hard it is to find a man who's interested in taking on a ready-made family. She hasn't had a date in months, poor thing. Spends her spare time going to her son's ath-letic events and taking her daughter to piano lessons. She seems to think divorced men who have custody of the children have an easier time of it. Apparently there are a lot more women willing to take on a ready-made family than there are men. In any event, having the kids doesn't seem to get in the way of a man's social life nearly as much as it gets in the way of a wom-an's."

Flynn cleared his throat and reached for his wine-glass. He watched Heather as she forked up her salad with almost vengeful enthusiasm. "We've never talked much about children," he remarked cautiously.

"Beth, the single parent I just mentioned, says," Heather broke in, "that men who get custody of the kids tend to remarry almost immediately. It seems they don't want to be saddled with the chores of single parenthood. They prefer to dump them on a new wife. Unfortunately single mothers don't always have the option of remarrying quickly. Hardly fair, is it?"

Flynn took a large swallow of wine and put his glass down with great precision. "Probably not, but don't you think it's going a little far to say that a divorced man who got custody of his child would turn right around and remarry just to get out from under the problems of being a single parent?"

"Oh, I don't know. Beth seems quite certain of her facts and she should know. She's had first-hand experience with divorce from the woman's point of view."

"That doesn't make her an expert on men who have been through a divorce."

"I think her observations are probably sound except for one thing."

Flynn eyed her through faintly narrowed lashes. "What's that?"

Heather, who was committed now and knew it, continued with a chatty casualness she was far from feeling. "Well, she seemed to think there was a vast array of females out there eager to take on not only a man who'd been through a divorce, but his kids, too."

"You don't think that's true?" Flynn asked very softly.

Heather pursed her lips thoughtfully. "Well, it may be a little true, but frankly, I don't know too many women who would fall all over themselves to take on a ready-made family. Think of all the problems. First there'd be the initial adjustment to marriage, which is hard enough. There'd be no real honeymoon period, would there? No chance to be alone with one's new husband. Then there would be the difficulties of trying to play mother to kids who weren't your own. Traumatic for all parties concerned, I'm sure. On top of everything else, a woman might resent the fact that she

had been married more as a convenience than anything else.''

"Don't you think,'' Flynn asked quietly, "that a
woman could learn to love a man's children even
though he might have had them by another woman?''

Heather felt her insides twist in painful tension. She
should never have started this, she thought wildly. It
had been the shock and initial anger that had driven
her this far. Neither was proving sufficiently strong to
keep her going. She'd set out tonight with the intention of forcing Flynn to be honest with her. She had
wanted to shake him out of his absolute certainty that
he had only to beckon and she would eventually come
back into his arms. She had wanted to let him know
she wouldn't be married just because he happened to
need a mother for his child.

"It would depend,'' she heard herself say in answer to his question.

"Depend on what?''

Heather felt as if she were suddenly floundering. It
was hard to imagine Flynn's son. Would the boy have
his father's tawny eyes or the eyes of a strange woman
Heather had never even met? Would he have his father's temperament or his mother's? "On whether she
felt loved for herself, I suppose. If she had some way
of knowing her husband had married her for love, not
because he just happened to need a mother for his
child, she might, eventually, be able to love both the
child and the man.''

"Heather,'' Flynn began, his voice raw as he put his
hand across the table to capture her fingers, "how
could a man caught in a situation such as you're de-
scribing ever prove himself? Honey, please listen to
me. I didn't realize you would feel like this. I guess I

just assumed that ... never mind. I have to explain something to you."

"It would be tricky, wouldn't it?" Heather said quietly.

He stared at her. "What would be tricky?"

"For the woman in question to figure out just why she had been married."

"Damn it, Heather, will you stop talking about some mythical female dreamed up by your friends at lunch? This is the real world and nothing's perfect. I'm sorry I'm not the untarnished knight in shining armor you're apparently searching for, but that doesn't mean that my reasons for asking you to marry me aren't legitimate. I want you. I know you're not ready to believe this yet, but I also love you. I'm doing my best to undo what I did eight months ago. Give me a chance, Heather."

She forced a dazzling smile. "Well, at least we don't have the added complications of fatherhood to worry about, do we? I mean, things would be so much more difficult if you had kids."

The tawny darkness of Flynn's eyes was filled with a gleaming determination. His hand tightened fiercely around hers. "Damn it, Heather, this isn't the way I wanted to handle this. I don't know how things got so screwed up. I thought I had everything organized and in order. Now it all seems to be falling apart."

"Flynn, I'm not sure I want to hear this."

"Just hush and listen to me, Heather Devaney. Believe me, you've done more than enough talking tonight. God knows, nothing has ever been easy with you."

"Except getting me into bed eight months ago."

Flynn ignored that and went on resolutely. "But I swear I didn't realize it was going to get this complicated. I want to tell you something important and I want your word you're not going to have hysterics."

"I never have hysterics. I don't know any woman who's ever had them. I think the idea of women having hysterics is a male myth."

"Then I want your word you won't fly off the handle when I tell you about my—"

"Flynn Rammage! Good to see you again. When are we going to get together for drinks?"

Both Flynn and Heather turned with a startled movement to see a tall, heavily built, middle-aged man standing beside the table. He was accompanied by an exquisitely dressed woman who appeared to be a few years younger. She smiled warmly at Heather while she waited for her husband to finish greeting Flynn. Heather knew at once the older woman hadn't missed the way Flynn's hand had been covering hers on the snowy tablecloth. She probably hadn't missed the intensity of his expression, either. Heather found herself vastly relieved by the interruption. Matters had been building to a climax and Heather wasn't sure how to stop the forces that had been set in motion.

Flynn recovered from his initial irritated surprise and quickly made introductions. "Heather, I want you to meet Carolyn and Harold Salisbury. Friends of mine. This is Heather Devaney."

"How do you do, Heather," Carolyn Salisbury said with charming grace. "It's good to see Flynn resuming his social life. He's been quite busy since he returned from Saudi Arabia a month and a half ago."

Harold Salisbury chuckled expansively, eyeing Heather with a knowing look. "Looks like Rammage is well on his way toward finding a mother for that boy of his, Carolyn. What do you think? Interested in the job, Heather?''

Heather didn't look at Flynn. She didn't dare. She sensed his utter stillness on the other side of the table, but she had her hands full trying to maintain a polite facade in front of his friends.

"I've never met Flynn's son," she murmured. "In fact, Flynn and I have never discussed children very much at all."

"That's because there were other things that had to be gotten out of the way first." Flynn's voice cut through the small silence like a knife. "Heather and I are still getting to know each other. We have a lot to talk about."

Harold Salisbury chuckled again. "And if that's not a hint, I don't know what is. Come on, Carolyn, let's leave these two alone. Give me a call one of these days, Rammage. We really should get together soon. I want to hear what you think of that new redevelopment project some idiot politician is proposing for downtown."

"Sure, Harold. I'll give you a call. Good night, Carolyn." Flynn was on his feet, his manner stiff but polite.

"Good night, Flynn. Nice to see you again. And nice to meet you, Heather." Carolyn Salisbury smiled benignly, a trace of amused understanding in her eyes as she allowed her husband to lead her off. Flynn sat down slowly, his eyes never leaving Heather's face.

"You already knew, didn't you," he finally said. It was a statement, not a question. "That's what all this was about tonight."

Heather stared down at her wineglass as she twisted the stem in her fingers. She suddenly wished the entire evening would simply disappear, but she knew it wouldn't. She'd never been that lucky around Flynn Rammage. "All what was about?"

"The bright clothes, the bright chatter, all that nonsense about dating divorced men who have kids. You were setting me up."

Her eyes jerked upward to meet his grim gaze. "I wanted you to tell me the truth. I was infuriated that you hadn't."

Flynn continued to contemplate her as though he had never quite seen her before. "How long have you known?"

"About your son? Since this afternoon. One of the women at lunch had heard her boss mention you and the fact that you'd recently gotten custody of the boy."

"His name is Jeremy." Flynn's tone was a little rough.

"Jeremy." Heather repeated the name softly to herself as the waiter materialized out of nowhere, carrying their dinner entrées. She tried to concentrate on the beautifully prepared tortellini in basil sauce that was being placed in front of her, but all she could think about was that now there was a name to go with Flynn's son. Jeremy.

"He's almost four years old," Flynn went on coolly as his prime rib was placed on the table in front of him. "In fact, he'll be turning four in a few days. He looks a lot like me."

"Is that right?" She didn't know what else to say. She picked up her fork and poked at the tortellini.

"So I owe this evening's scene to some gossiping friend of yours," Flynn mused. He used his knife to slice into the prime rib in a quick, brutal manner.

"Beth wasn't gossiping! She assumed I knew all about the boy."

"Jeremy."

"All about Jeremy," Heather repeated unhappily. His insistence on making her use his son's name was deliberate and she knew it. He wanted to force her to think of the boy as an individual, not just a vague, unknown child who could be lumped together in her mind with every other child in the world. "This evening's scene, as you call it, came about because I was furious about being kept in the dark. I wanted to force you to admit exactly what you were up to when you asked me to marry you. You said that regardless of whatever else you've done, you've never lied to me. Well, as far as I'm concerned, keeping Jeremy a secret comes damn close."

"You're acting as if you'd just learned I've got another lover instead of a son."

Heather closed her eyes in brief despair. "You don't understand how I feel, do you? You never did understand me. It was a mistake to even think about trying to rebuild what we once had. As usual, you're just looking for the most expedient way of getting what you want. Last time around it was a roll in the sack and a chance to punish a woman for what your wife had done. This time you happen to need a mother for... for Jeremy."

His knife still gripped in one fist, Flynn suddenly leaned forward. His eyes were relentless and accusing. "And what is it you're looking for, Heather? The perfect man who has been kept under glass for the past thirty or forty years, untouched by life? Someone who hasn't made any mistakes? Who's always treated you like a princess? Who comes to you with a clean slate and no embarrassing encumbrances such as an ex-wife and a kid?''

"Sounds wonderful," she shot back fiercely, angered by the way he was trying to put her on the defensive. He was the one on trial this evening as far as she was concerned. Trust Flynn to try to reverse things. "He would be someone with whom I could start fresh. Someone with whom I could build a future."

"Well, good luck finding him, because I doubt that he's out there." Flynn sat back and attacked his meat again. His full attention seemed to be on dissecting the prime rib. "What's more, I'm not sure you've got much to offer such a paragon, even if you do succeed in locating him."

Heather paled under the insult. She felt as if he'd struck her. Wide-eyed, she stared at Flynn, her trembling fingers thrust into a small, tight fist in her lap. "As usual," she whispered, "you've had the last word. You were always so good with words. I'd like to leave now, Flynn. I can't possibly eat another bite."

His head came up abruptly, eyes narrowing as he took in the expression on her face. "Oh, hell," he grated, setting down his knife. "I didn't mean that the way it sounded."

"Didn't you? I think you made yourself quite clear. Will you take me home, or shall I call a cab?"

"Heather," he growled, "listen to me. I was angry."

"I'm sick of being the one you turn on when you're angry," she snapped.

"I don't like being set up. You should have asked about Jeremy the minute you found out about him. There was no need for all this game playing tonight. And as for what I said a minute ago, I'll be glad to explain what I meant."

"Forget it."

"The hell I will. You seem to want a perfect romantic illusion, a fairy-tale affair, not a real marriage. Marriage means a home and a husband who might not always treat you perfectly. In this case it also means getting involved with a child who isn't your own. You're going to have to bring a lot of love and tolerance and commitment into a marriage, Heather. If you can't offer those three things then you haven't got much to offer any man, let alone a paragon such as the one you say you want."

"And what do I get in return?" she asked coldly.

"Love and tolerance and commitment." Flynn's face relaxed and a measure of indulgent tenderness appeared in his eyes.

"I think you're the one who's looking for a paragon," Heather remarked with artificial calm. She put her napkin on the table. "Beth assures me there are a lot of female paragons just waiting to take you up on your offer. Good luck finding one. Can we go now, please?"

"No. I haven't finished my prime rib."

"Then I'll phone for a taxi." She started to get to her feet but was halted by the cool command in his next words.

"Sit down."

Heather fumed silently. Flynn hadn't raised his voice, but that didn't lessen the impact. She began to understand why he was so good at his job. "There isn't much else to say, is there? We've insulted each other enough for one evening.''

"You started it,'' he informed her with a startling hint of humor. "I was on my best behavior until you deliberately pushed me into a corner.''

Heather discovered she wasn't prepared for the switch from masculine irritation to indulgent amusement. "Why didn't you tell me about...about Jeremy?'' She still found it difficult to say the boy's name. On some level, Heather knew, she didn't want to give the child a real identity. It was easier not to be interested in him if she kept him a totally unknown quantity in her mind.

"Strange as this may sound, I was holding him in reserve in case I blew my chance with you,'' Flynn explained quite calmly. "I figured if I messed up badly, I could always bring in the big guns, namely him. I told myself that you might be able to resist me, but you probably wouldn't be able to resist my son.''

"Was that assumption based on some ridiculous theory that all women go crazy over babies?''

"Nope. I knew better than that. I'm fully aware that not all women go crazy over babies. My ex-wife is a good example.''

Heather shifted restlessly, moving her gaze around the room. "I'd rather not talk about your ex-wife, Flynn.''

"I think it's time we did. While we're at it, I think we'll get a few other details out of the way, too. Are you going to eat any more of that tortellini?''

"No.'' She'd probably disgrace herself if she tried, Heather thought. Her stomach was in knots. "The only thing I want right now is to go home.''

"All right," Flynn agreed. "I've done about as much damage as I can do on this prime rib. Let's go."

Relieved that the painful evening was finally about to come to an end, Heather waited impatiently as Flynn paid the bill. When that task was finished she turned to lead the way toward the door of the restaurant. He was forced to take a couple of long strides in order to catch up with her just as she pushed open the glass doors and stepped out into the pleasantly warm darkness. Flynn grabbed for and caught hold of her arm.

"Nothing like an eager woman," he growled, reaching for his car keys as he kept a firm grip on Heather.

Heather overlooked the two-edged remark as they walked to the far end of the parking lot. Flynn had a habit of parking his precious car as far away from other cars as possible to protect it from the dreaded parking-lot dent. Privately Heather had never seen much sense in owning a car that had to be treated so carefully. "You do understand that the reason I'm in such a rotten mood tonight is because I feel like I'm the one who's been set up, don't you, Flynn?" she demanded as he deposited her into the passenger seat of the Porsche.

He didn't answer, but closed the door gently on the question. A moment later he opened the door on the driver's side and moved in beside her. "First I'll explain what was going on in my life eight months ago," he announced.

Heather sighed and leaned her head back against the seat as Flynn turned the car out of the parking lot. She told herself she didn't want to hear what was coming, but she couldn't think of any easy way to avoid it. She sat in mute silence while Flynn began his explanations.

"It wasn't just the divorce that had me in a flaming rage at the time I met you, Heather. In some ways the divorce was a relief. Cheryl and I hadn't been getting along well for a couple of years and things were getting worse rapidly. I can't say I was pleased to learn about her affair with her instructor, but I wasn't exactly surprised, either. The divorce went through without a hitch. Neither of us wanted to contest it. What didn't go through the way I had assumed it would was the matter of custody."

"You went to court to try to get custody of Jeremy?" Heather asked in surprise.

Flynn nodded in the shadows, his face grim. "I didn't think Cheryl would ever bother to ask for him. He was the cause of a lot of our problems in the first place. She hadn't wanted kids. I did. Like a couple of fools we hadn't really discussed the matter before marriage. It came as a shock to me that she had no intention of having children. I guess it came as an equally strong shock to her that I wanted them. For the first couple of years of the marriage we could shelve the whole problem and pretend it didn't exist. But as time went on, I started pushing her to agree to try for a baby. She refused. Everything we had going between us started getting very shaky at that point. She felt trapped and angry. I felt exactly the same way. Then she got pregnant."

"What a mess," Heather said with a sigh.

"It was an accident. The precautions Cheryl had been using failed. After we realized what had happened, she started talking about an abortion. I panicked and begged her not to go through with it. She finally gave in and decided to have the baby. To give her credit, I honestly think she tried to make the best of the situation. But after Jeremy was born it became clear that she had been right from the beginning. She wasn't cut out to be a mother."

"Some women aren't, just as some men don't seem to be cut out to be fathers."

Flynn's hand tightened on the wheel. "I know that now. Cheryl and I were mismatched from the beginning. At any rate, after Jeremy came things began going downhill rapidly. She hired someone to look after him all day, and then in the evenings she left him with me while she signed up for every night class she could find at the university. It wasn't long before she fell for one of her teachers, although it took me a while to realize what was going on all those evenings when Jeremy and I were home alone. Nothing like keeping busy changing diapers and fixing bottles to prevent you from thinking about what your wife is doing behind your back."

Heather heard a trace of the old bitterness in his words and stirred uneasily. Perhaps divorced people never did get rid of all traces of the anger and resentment that came out of the breakup of a family. "Flynn, maybe we shouldn't talk about this."

"No, it's about time we did. Should have thrashed the whole thing out earlier. I finally got my head above the diapers and the bottles long enough to come to my senses. I confronted Cheryl and she admitted she was in love with someone else. She wanted a divorce. I told her to get out and that I intended to keep Jeremy. I didn't expect her to go after him in court."

"Why not?" Heather asked quietly. "It was the only way she could punish you. She knew you wanted him so she decided to take him from you."

Flynn shot her an appraising glance. "It was a totally irrational act."

"So was your treatment of me eight months ago," she reminded him. "People tend to act irrationally when they're angry. She probably blamed you for forcing her to have Jeremy in the first place."

Flynn drew a deep breath, as if trying to hold on to his temper. "I fought for Jeremy with everything I had. I got the best lawyers money could buy. I figured there was hope because in some recent cases fathers have been awarded custody. But Cheryl played the role of the brokenhearted mother about to be torn from her son. And most judges are still a little old-fashioned under the surface."

"She got custody."

"Heather, I had just lost Jeremy for good about the time you took that job at Con-Struct. I'd never felt so trapped, so helpless and so frustrated in my life. I knew Cheryl didn't want him, yet there was absolutely nothing I could do. I had to stand aside and let her take him to live with her and her lover. The first thing they did was move to California. I couldn't even see Jeremy conveniently on weekends or after work. I was mad at every female in the world. I had been faithful to Cheryl, so after the divorce I didn't have a little black book full of telephone numbers. Hell, for a while I wasn't even interested in getting involved with anyone. Besides, most of the women who knew me were smart enough to keep their distance."

"But not me."

"No," he agreed softly, "not you. But I think you saw some of the rage in me, didn't you, Heather?"

"Yes," she admitted, her eyes still on the passing lights. "I saw it."

"And you looked past it. You took your chances with me because you saw something else besides the pent-up anger, didn't you?"

"I deluded myself. Sheer stupidity."

"No," Flynn said flatly. "You fell in love with me. I knew it at the time. Knew it and hated myself for letting it happen even while I tried to convince myself you were just another flighty female who deserved what she got. I never meant to take you to bed more than once or twice, Heather. I just wanted to prove I could love 'em and leave 'em.

"Two weeks after the affair started I woke up one morning and realized that things were getting out of control. I was falling in love with you and I panicked. If you want to know the truth, I was angry, too. I'd made a mistake somewhere along the line. I'd let you get to me. That hadn't been part of the plan at all. I had to get away, so I jumped at the Saudi job. But no matter how hard I tried, I couldn't get you off my mind.

"Then one day I got a letter from Cheryl. She was tired of punishing me, it seems. More than that, her new husband wasn't exactly thrilled to find himself raising another man's son. The bottom line was that Cheryl had never really wanted kids in the first place. She told me she was willing to give Jeremy back to me. No strings attached. I rushed home from the Middle East and grabbed my son."

"I see," Heather whispered, not knowing what else to say. "So you got your son back and then you started looking around for someone who would be willing to mother him, and you immediately remembered me."

"I'd never forgotten you, Heather," Flynn said softly. "Even if I hadn't gotten Jeremy I would have shown up on your doorstep sooner or later. I don't care what your gossiping friends claim. A man doesn't marry a woman just to acquire a mother for his child. He can hire housekeepers and nannies if he's just looking for domestic help. I want you for my wife in every sense of the word. I wanted to convince you of that fact before I introduced you to Jeremy."

"Because you were afraid that if you hadn't properly seduced me first, I might take to my heels when I discovered I was expected to take on the task of becoming an instant mother?"

"No," Flynn said as he parked the Porsche in front of her house. "I didn't tell you about Jeremy in the beginning because I wanted to make sure you loved me for myself. I already know you're going to love Jeremy. I didn't want you agreeing to marry me because of him unless there was no other way to get you."

# Five

Heather's immediate reaction to Flynn's comment about wanting to be loved for himself was a cruelly unsettling sensation of looking into a dark mirror. He had been intent on making sure of her, while she had wanted to find some way of making sure of him. It was ironic. It was also unnerving.

"I think you took an awful lot for granted, Flynn." She opened her car door and stepped out onto the sidewalk.

Flynn pursued her up the walk to the front door, taking the keys from her hand and inserting them into the lock. "I didn't take too much for granted. I'm very sure about us, Heather. I've had eight months to think it all through. But I'll admit that I haven't handled this situation as well as I could have. I ought to have told you about Jeremy right from the start."

"You certainly should have." She pushed past him into the security of her own home.

"I'll admit I screwed up, Heather, but that doesn't change anything. You and I have to work this out and that's all there is to it."

"I'm not so sure." She flipped on a light as she dropped her purse on the wobbly card table. "Personally, I think the situation is beyond fixing. What's more..." Her voice trailed off as she glanced into the shadowed kitchen and saw the back door closing with an unnatural silence.

Heather screamed, more in sheer outrage than any real fear. She was too furious to be frightened. Hitching up the narrow hem of the red dress, she raced into the darkness of the kitchen.

"Heather! What the hell?" Flynn came after her, reaching out to grab her wrist just as she would have yanked open the door. "What the devil's the matter with you?"

"There was someone in here!" she panted, trying to wriggle free of his grasp. "In my house. An intruder in *my house*. He went out the back door as we came in the front. Let go of me, Flynn."

"Don't be stupid. Call the cops. I'll see if I can find him," Flynn declared. "And whatever you do, don't get any ideas about going after him." He gave her a push toward the phone on the kitchen counter and then he was through the back door.

Heather stared after him for a few seconds and then she grabbed the phone. *An intruder in her new home.* It was an outrage. It was a violation. She'd get a gun. And a dog. A big dog. How dared anyone come into her home without her permission? Her hands were shaking with rage as she dialed.

* * *

A long time later Flynn lounged on the carpet in Heather's sparsely furnished living room, propped on his elbow, a glass of brandy on the floor in front of him. He had disdained sitting on one of the unsteady folding chairs that went with the card table, not at all sure it would hold his weight.

He watched Heather with a hooded gaze, not quite certain how to deal with her. She was still high-strung and restless, even though she'd had a couple of sips from the glass of brandy he had poured for her after the cops had left. She sat cross-legged a short distance away, her expressive features reflecting her inner turmoil.

"This sort of thing always comes as a shock, Heather. Be glad you didn't have anything in here worth stealing. It was probably just as much of a shock to the intruder when he discovered he'd broken into a house that was practically empty."

"There was my stereo. He didn't even touch it."

"Maybe we got home before he had a chance to take it."

"He was right here in my house. Walking around on my floors, touching my things. He had no right to be here!" She took another swallow of brandy and glared defiantly at Flynn.

"I know," Flynn said gently.

"Are you sure you didn't see any sign at all of him while you were outside?" she prodded for about the hundredth time.

"Heather, most of your backyard is in gravel. It doesn't show any footprints. It was impossible to tell which direction he'd gone." It was about the hundredth time he'd made the explanation. The cops hadn't done any better than Flynn had.

"I know, I know." She was silent for a moment, thinking of how frustrating it all was. The cops had said they'd keep an eye out for any strangers in the neighborhood, but they hadn't offered much hope of capturing the intruder unless he continued to operate in the area. "I should have gone after him myself. We lost him while I took valuable time trying to explain to you what I'd seen."

"How far do you think you'd have gotten in those high heels you were wearing?"

Moodily Heather glanced down at the jeans and loafers she'd put on after the police had left. "Not far," she admitted with a forlorn sigh.

Flynn swirled the brandy in the bottom of his glass before saying in a very neutral tone, "Why don't you come out to my place and spend the night there? You're bound to be nervous here in this house all by yourself after what's happened. Perfectly natural reaction."

"I'm not nervous. I'm mad."

His mouth tilted briefly at the corners. "I can tell."

She glared at him. "This is my home, Flynn. The first house I've ever owned. I've spent years saving up the down payment. I've invested hundreds of dollars in repairs and I've got plans for all kinds of modifications. Now some intruder thinks he can just walk in here and take anything he wants."

"It's all right, Heather," Flynn tried to say soothingly. "There was nothing for him to take except the stereo, and he left that behind. Apparently he didn't see any antique value in that old card table or the few things you've got in the kitchen."

"I was going to buy a new television next month," Heather explained sadly. "I decided to wait awhile before getting it. I'd rather put the money toward new wallpaper."

"Didn't you have any furniture of your own in your old apartment?"

Heather shook her head. "I rented almost everything. What I didn't rent, I had bought secondhand at yard sales. I didn't want to bring much of it with me. I was just going to put good stuff into this place. I was saving up for exactly what I wanted. I wanted everything to be just right in my first home. I'm going to start fresh here, Flynn, with everything from the drapes to the sofa."

"Well, if you're going to stay here for any length of time the first thing you'd better invest in is decent locks," Flynn said bluntly.

Her head came up in astonishment. "What do you mean, *if* I'm going to stay here for any length of time?"

He took a swallow of brandy. "You know what I mean. Sooner or later you're going to move in with me as my wife. This place is only a temporary home for you, Heather, and you know it."

"For pete's sake! I have just been robbed. All I can think about is the violation of my home and you're sitting there telling me not to worry because I'll soon be marrying you!"

"You weren't robbed," Flynn pointed out once again. "There was nothing here for him to take. I know this isn't the time to talk about our future. You're obviously badly shaken. I'm sorry I mentioned the subject, but that doesn't change anything.

One of these days you're going to marry me. I came back to the States to collect both you and Jeremy.''

"You came back to the States to collect Jeremy, period. It was after you got him that you decided I might be useful."

Flynn kept his temper with obvious difficulty. "Well, I've got him. It won't be long before I have you." The hard edge of his voice abruptly softened. "Come here," he went on coaxingly, leaning over to pull her tense body into the circle of his arm. He smiled down into her mutinous hazel eyes. "Take it easy. You're as stiff as a board." He began massaging the muscles of her neck and shoulders.

Heather wasn't sure she wanted to be soothed by anyone, let alone Flynn Rammage. She was still trying to deal with what had happened that evening, all of it, not just the fact that someone had invaded her privacy. But Flynn's big hands were amazingly persuasive. Before she knew what was happening, she began to relax under his touch.

Flynn didn't speak again until he felt some of the tension in Heather finally begin to dissolve. He was pleased that his touch was having that effect on her. When he thought the time was right, he spoke cautiously.

"I'd like you to meet Jeremy." Almost instantly Heather's muscles began to tighten beneath his hands.

"I don't see the point," she muttered. But she was fighting a rearguard action and she knew it.

"Now that you know about him, you'll have to meet him," Flynn said casually. "You know that, Heather. Why not come out to the house with me tonight?"

"I've told you. I want to stay here."

"All right. I'm not going to force you into anything."

"Gee, thanks," she muttered scornfully.

"But sooner or later you're going to face the fact that what I'm offering is exactly what you want."

She tilted one eyebrow and slanted him a glance. "Is that right?"

"'Fraid so." His fingers never stopped their soothing action on her shoulders. "Just look at the facts, Heather. You're a woman who wants a home so badly she can taste it. You want a man to love, and you've got the built-in generosity and capacity to love a child, too. You don't want to just live in a house. You want to make a home. A real home."

"What makes you so sure?"

"I was sure from the first. That's probably one of the things that attracted me to you in the beginning, even though I was too mad at the world to treat you with the respect you deserved. Things have changed, honey."

"They certainly have," she agreed, staring unhappily at the old, threadbare carpet.

Flynn pulled her back against him, enveloping her in the warmth of his body as he wrapped his arms around her waist. "Don't run from what you really want just because you're angry at me for the way I've handled things. Give us both a chance again, Heather."

"You told me earlier I didn't want the responsibilities of a ready-made family," she reminded him harshly. "You told me I was looking for a perfect man and a perfect romantic situation."

Flynn groaned and tightened his grip around her waist. "I was angry. I wanted to shake you up a bit for what you did to me this evening."

"I didn't do anything to you except force you to tell me the truth. I'm still not sure you would have done it if your friends hadn't stopped by our table when they did."

"I was going to tell you, Heather. But I wanted to do it in my own time and in my own way."

"After you'd hustled me into marriage? I can see it now. On our wedding night you could have poured a glass of champagne, smiled charmingly and said, 'Oh, by the way, honey, there's a little something I forgot to mention. You're going to be an instant mother.'"

"I wouldn't have done it that way and you know it."

"No, I don't know it. Look at the way you ended our so-called relationship eight months ago. No warning, no clues, just a casual goodbye and instructions not to make things awkward at the office until after you'd left town." Heather's fingers clenched into small fists at the memory.

Flynn caught hold of one of her hands and wrapped it securely in his big palm. His touch was warm and gentle and firm. He bent his head to kiss the curve of her throat. "I was a bastard. I admit it. But I've given you the only excuse I have to give. I was in a cold-blooded rage because I'd just lost my son to a woman I knew didn't really love him. I was looking for someone to punish and you got in the way. I'm sorry, Heather. God only knows how sorry I am. For the first couple of months in Saudi I worked night and day trying to forget the whole mess. You and Jeremy both haunted me. I drove everyone around me crazy. Even men who've worked for me for years were walking on eggs every time they got within shouting distance of me. It took two months before I'd calmed down enough to become reasonably rational. As my world began to clear I realized I had to come back for you. But I still wasn't back to normal. I needed time and I knew it. I figured another couple of months of hard work would get rid of the devils that were driving me. Believe me, for an American working in that part of the world there's no other way to exorcise devils except with hard work. Life is pretty restricted there.''

"If you're expecting me to feel sorry for you because of the limited nightlife in the Middle East, you can forget it," Heather told him irritably.

"I'm not expecting anything. I'm trying to finish my explanations and get them behind me. Listen, honey, because I'm not going through them again. After tonight we go forward, not backward in this relationship. As I was saying, a couple of months into the assignment I finally started coming to my senses. I missed you badly and I was furious with myself for having wrecked the one good thing I'd found amid the ruins. I sent word back to the home office here in Tucson."

"What word?"

"That I wanted to contact you. I figured it was going to be a bit tricky because I knew I'd hurt you."

"I survived."

Flynn nodded against her hair. "So I see. At any rate, I was stunned to hear you'd quit Con-Struct. I'd assumed that with me out of the country there was no reason for you to run."

"You thought I'd just hang around the office and live on false hopes until you decided to return? Come on, Flynn. I've got some pride."

"I know." He sighed. "Too much."

"You say that only because it's getting in the way of what you want at the moment. If the situation was reversed, how much pride do you think you would have had?"

"There's no point talking about it," he told her deliberately. "I'm going to finish this story and get it behind me. As I said, I contacted the home office and learned you'd quit. No forwarding address. I made a few attempts to locate you, but it was hard trying to coordinate that kind of thing from so far away. No one knew where you'd gone. Personnel said no one had even asked for your references."

"When I applied to Talon I specifically requested that my former employer not be contacted," Heather informed him aloofly. "I was afraid it might cost me the job, but Talon was very understanding."

"Yeah, well, Talon's understanding attitude cost me a lot of time and misery. By the time I'd finally given up trying to locate you long distance I was four months into the job. I figured another two months would take care of the business end of things and then I'd be free to come back to the States and find you. Shortly after that I got the letter from Cheryl saying I could have Jeremy. Three weeks after that I had him. It took the poor kid a while to settle down again after I brought him back to Tucson. And it took me a while to adjust to being a single parent. When I thought I finally had everything under control again, I came looking for you. You're not even in the phone book."

"Unlisted number," she mumbled, wishing she could tune out his explanations. She knew from past experience just how persuasive Flynn Rammage could be when he tried. He had always been able to seduce her with words.

"I went to your old apartment, but you'd already moved out."

"The lease was up on my apartment and I didn't want to renew because I knew I would be moving into my new house soon. I stayed with a friend until the deal on this place closed."

Flynn's arms tensed around her. "A male friend?"

"Is that any business of yours?"

"No," he admitted, his voice raw, "but where you're concerned I feel possessive. I have a hunch I'm going to feel that way for the rest of my life."

Heather stirred in his embrace and exhaled heavily. "I stayed with a friend from work. A female friend."

"Thank you for telling me," he said quietly. "I know that for the past few months I haven't had any rights where you're concerned."

"Nothing's changed, Flynn," she declared stoutly. "You still don't have any rights."

His hands flattened on her stomach as he pulled her deeper into his warmth. "You don't hate me, Heather. We both know that."

"Do we?"

There was just a trace of satisfaction buried in his words as he said, "I knew you didn't hate me when you opened the door to me a few days ago. I saw the look in your eyes before you recovered from the shock of seeing me. There was no hatred in them."

Heather didn't want to ask what he had seen in her face during those brief, unguarded seconds. "You're

right. I don't hate you," she admitted wearily. "If I
did I wouldn't have been going out with you for the
past few days. But that doesn't mean I'm ready to pick
up where we left off. Quite frankly, it was a hell of a
shock learning that you're in the market for a mother
for your son."

"Heather, I'm in the market, as you put it, for a
*wife*, not just a mother for Jeremy. I'll admit I can't
separate one from the other, not now that I've got
Jeremy to consider. You can understand that. I know
you can. Don't try to put up impossible barriers between us."

Heather heard the warning in his words and tried to
ease herself away from his close grasp. "I don't think
this is the best time to discuss our relationship, such as
it is, Flynn. I've had enough surprises to deal with today. It's time you went home."

"I think you should come with me. You're bound
to be nervous staying here by yourself. Besides, tomorrow is Saturday. You can spend the day with Jeremy and me. It'll give you a chance to get to know my
son."

"You expect me to be overcome by latent maternal
instincts the moment I set eyes on Jeremy?" Heather
asked bleakly as she rose to her knees.

Flynn met her eyes, but he didn't respond to the
challenge. "Now that you know about him, you
should meet him," he said steadily.

"I don't think—" Heather broke off abruptly as the
telephone in the kitchen rang sharply. Frowning, she
scrambled to her feet and hurried to answer it. The
voice on the other end of the line was female and it
sounded anxious.

"I'm calling for Flynn Rammage, please."

Startled, Heather murmured agreement and held the phone against her shirt. "For you, Flynn."

He frowned, getting to his feet immediately and striding into the kitchen. He took the phone with an abrupt gesture.

"Rammage here." A pause. "It's okay, Nancy. That's why I left this number for you. Now tell me exactly what's wrong." Another pause. "All right, I'll be right home. Stop worrying, I'm sure it's nothing serious. I'll call his pediatrician from here. Right. I'll be there as soon as I can." Flynn hung up the phone, his face set in serious lines. When he turned to look at Heather all trace of sensuality had disappeared from his expression.

"What's wrong?" she asked hesitantly.

"That was my baby-sitter. She says Jeremy has started running a fever and complaining about his stomach. Can I use your phone to call his doctor?"

"Of course." Heather moved to stand on the other side of the counter, watching with an odd feeling of curiosity as Flynn dialed the pediatrician's after-hours number. He got through almost immediately and there was a succinct, urgent conversation. When it was done Flynn looked a little relieved but still serious.

"He says it sounds like a stomach flu that's been going around. He's phoning in a prescription to a drugstore that stays open until midnight. I'll pick up the medicine on my way home. He says if Jeremy's not showing any improvement by noon tomorrow I'm to call again." Flynn turned away, heading for the living room and the jacket he'd left on one of the rickety folding chairs. "Sorry about this, Heather. One of the hazards of trying to be a parent and conduct a social life at the same time. I've got to get home." He slung the jacket over his shoulder and fished his keys out of his pocket. "Listen, about what happened here tonight. Try not to worry about it. I'm sure that guy won't be back. He knows now there's nothing here to steal. He'll realize the cops will be keeping an eye on the neighborhood."

Heather made up her mind in a quick, intuitive rush. She slipped out from behind the counter. "I'm coming with you."

Flynn looked startled. "What?"

"You heard me. I'll be right with you. I just want to throw some things in a bag." She was already hurrying down the hall to her bedroom. Flynn followed her, his voice urgent.

"Heather, you don't want to come back to the house with me tonight. You said so. I'm going to have a sick kid on my hands, and believe me, that isn't one of life's really fun experiences."

"Are you canceling the invitation you issued earlier this evening?" She didn't bother to glance at him as she grabbed a shirt from the closet and some underwear from a drawer.

"Well, no, but you didn't want to come with me then and I don't see . . ."

"I've changed my mind." She stuffed the clothing into a small bag and yanked at the bag's zipper. With a determined smile, she spun around. "I'm ready. All I need is my toothbrush. If you'll kindly get out of the way?"

Flynn's eyes darkened as she wriggled past him to get into her bathroom. "Heather, this isn't the way I wanted it to be the first time you met Jeremy."

"Afraid he'll make a bad impression?" She unzipped the bag far enough to add the toothbrush and a couple of other items from the medicine chest.

"Heather, be reasonable. He's sick, damn it."

"Earlier you accused me of wanting a perfect arrangement with a man who wasn't divorced or encumbered with kids from a previous marriage. You implied I wasn't interested in the reality of family life, just a romantic image of it. Okay, I'm willing to take a look at reality. Let's go."

Flynn glared at her. "This isn't the way to get introduced to it. Believe me."

"Now who's trying to hide reality behind a rosy facade?" she challenged. Heather slung the soft travel bag over her shoulder. "Hadn't we better be on our way? You have to pick up that medicine and your baby-sitter will be getting nervous."

Flynn swore softly and turned around to stalk down the hall. "All right, if that's the way you want it, come on. But I warn you I'm not going to be able to drive you back home if you change your mind in a couple of hours. If you come with me tonight you'll be stuck with Jeremy and me until morning."

"I know." She trotted after him, turning out lights as she went. At the front door Heather cast a quick, anxious eye around her little house and then firmly closed and locked the door. Flynn was right. Whoever had intruded tonight was unlikely to return. With a sigh she pocketed her keys and hurried down the front walk. Flynn was already in the Porsche, starting the engine. She opened the passenger door and slipped in beside him.

"This is a lousy idea, you know," he told her as he pulled away from the curb.

"Going home with you? It was your idea," she replied innocently.

"I had no idea Jeremy was going to be ill."

"Reality, Flynn, remember?" Heather sat back in the seat and wondered what on earth had led her into such an impulsive decision. Earlier in the evening she'd had absolutely no intention of going home with Flynn. A part of her, she knew, was almost afraid to meet Jeremy. She didn't want to add a face and a personality to the name. It was safer to keep Jeremy an unknown quantity in the difficult equation she faced. But when she'd seen Flynn make the abrupt shift from would-be lover to concerned parent, something within Heather gave. Suddenly she had to know the little boy who had such an influence over Flynn Rammage.

Flynn drove swiftly through the desert night, his concentration split between worrying about Jeremy and wondering how the hell he'd found himself bringing Heather back to face a sick kid and a sleepless night. This wasn't the way he'd wanted it to be at all.

He found the drugstore without any trouble and left Heather in the Porsche while he went quickly inside to collect the medicine. When he came out he glanced at Heather's calm face through the windshield. The harsh parking lot lights revealed almost nothing of her inner emotions and Flynn wondered grimly what she was thinking.

It occurred to Flynn as he got back into the car that Heather might have decided to come back to the house with him because she wanted to see his son under less than ideal circumstances. She flung the word "reality" into his face, but maybe she was secretly hoping a dose of it was exactly what she needed to help her sever the last of the frayed bonds that bound her to him. The ideal of motherhood might hold an intrinsic appeal for a woman with a nesting instinct as strong as Heather's, but the reality of finding herself dealing with another woman's sick, fretful child might be an altogether different matter.

Flynn shoved the car into gear and told himself that it was too late now. The die was cast.

Reality awaited.

Heather found herself half eager and half wary as Flynn left the main road and turned into a residential area situated in the hills above Tucson. She had never been to his home. During the brief affair eight months ago Flynn had always come back to her apartment. He'd never invited her to his house. She'd wondered later if that was because his own home held too many bitter memories.

There was little street lighting, but the moon was almost full, and it revealed a low, sprawling, modern, southwestern-style structure that displayed unmistakable signs of affluence. Before Heather could get a good look, Flynn had parked the Porsche in the circular drive and was already half out of the car. He headed toward the double front doors without waiting to see if Heather was following.

The front doors opened to reveal a girl of about sixteen or seventeen dressed in jeans and a striped pullover. She looked relieved to see her employer.

"He's resting now, Mr. Rammage, but he's been getting more and more fretful."

"How's the fever?" Flynn asked.

"It's not getting any worse, but he's definitely too warm. Every time he wakes up he says his stomach hurts."

"Has he thrown up?"

"No, not yet." The girl cast a quick glance at Heather, who was walking toward the door with her bag. She smiled. "Sorry to wreck your evening."

"Don't be silly," Heather said calmly. "You did the right thing by calling Flynn. My name is Heather Devaney, by the way. Shall I stay with Jeremy while you drive Nancy home?" she added, glancing at Flynn.

"Usually I wake him up and take him with me while I drive her home," Flynn said uncertainly. Then he seemed to come to a decision. "But that probably isn't a good idea tonight. All right, Heather. You keep an eye on him. I'll be back in ten or fifteen minutes. Ready, Nancy?"

The teenager nodded. "I'll get my books."

Heather followed Nancy into the house. "Where's Jeremy?"

"In the last bedroom down the hall. He's sleeping now."

Heather nodded. "Fine. Good night, Nancy."

"Good night, Miss Devaney."

Flynn glanced inside from the door where he was waiting for Nancy. "Sure you're going to be all right here alone with Jeremy for a few minutes?"

"I'll manage."

He eyed her speculatively for a moment and then shut the door behind himself and Nancy without a word.

Heather glanced around the striking living room as she set down her bag. She knew instinctively that the interior design was the work of Flynn's ex-wife. Heather made her way toward the hall that led to the bedrooms, examining the slick, sleek, Los Angeles look of the house.

Black lacquer, glass, slate, leather and mirrors dominated the rooms. There was an oddly formal, sophisticated look to the furnishings that didn't seem to mesh with either the southwestern architecture or a house that was home to a small boy and his father.

Heather smiled ruefully as she stepped quietly into a bedroom and found herself looking down at the small form huddled under the sheet. She knew she was overreacting to the interior design work because it was a tangible expression of the other woman who had shared Flynn's life. Here in Flynn's home Heather was surrounded by his ex-wife's presence.

But the most blatant expression of that presence took the shape of a small boy with dark hair. Even as Heather stood bent over Jeremy to test his forehead with her palm he opened his eyes. For an instant he stared up at her with dazed, uncertain tawny brown eyes.

"Where's Daddy?" And then Jeremy Rammage sat up with a jerk and proceeded to throw up all over Heather's loafers.

# Six

Flynn walked through the front door ten minutes later. Busy with Jeremy in the bathroom, Heather heard him and called his name.

"In here, Flynn!"

"What the hell?" Flynn appeared in the bathroom doorway, taking in the evidence in one quick glance. An oddly chagrined expression flickered briefly in his eyes as he pulled the bottle of medicine out of the bag. He slid a quick glance at Heather, who was standing barefoot on the gray rug as she gently helped a feverish, restless Jeremy rinse out his mouth. "Sorry," Flynn muttered brusquely.

"Hardly your fault," Heather observed dryly. "He's been asking for you."

"Daddy!" Jeremy held out his arms. "My tummy hurts."

"I can tell. Don't worry, I've got some stuff to take care of that. As soon as we change your pajamas we'll give you some." Flynn ruffled his son's hair affectionately and then began feeding the boy's little arms and legs into the clean pair of pajamas Heather had found.

With a groggy indifference Jeremy submitted to being re-dressed. By the time Flynn had finished and had convinced him to swallow the medicine Jeremy was almost asleep.

Heather stood aside, watching as Flynn carried the boy back to bed. Then she rinsed off her loafers and wiped them dry with a paper towel. There was still the mess on the carpet, she reminded herself, and rummaged around under the marble countertop until she found a sponge and some more paper towels.

Flynn glanced at her with a quick frown as she walked back into the bedroom. "Here," he said gruffly, "I'll do that. Go on out into the living room. I'll be out in a few minutes."

Shrugging, Heather nodded and walked out. It was obvious Flynn didn't want her being exposed to the less pleasant aspects of motherhood, she thought with amusement. At least, not right off. She ambled out into the living room and sat down gingerly on an elegant leather sofa she knew must have cost several thousand dollars. A few minutes later Flynn reappeared.

"I'll get us some brandy," he announced, running a hand through his hair. "We never got a chance to finish the glass we started at your place."

Curious about the kitchen, Heather got to her feet and trailed him into a high-tech, gleaming wonder that looked like something out of a magazine.

"Are you a gourmet chef?" she asked, eyeing the surroundings.

"Hardly." He opened a glass-paned cupboard door and removed two snifters. "I can handle eggs and hamburgers. Both of which Jeremy likes, fortunately."

"But all this fancy cookware..." Heather began, letting the sentence trail into extinction as she indicated the exotic kitchen.

"Cheryl was into the latest food fads," Flynn said shortly. "She liked to entertain."

"I see." Even the kitchen belonged to the absent Cheryl. Well, it made sense, Heather told herself. A woman naturally held sway in her own home, even after she'd left. Heather clasped her arms under her breasts in a small, unconsciously defensive gesture.

Flynn watched her, reading the faint signs of withdrawal with unerring accuracy. "Here," he growled, shoving the brandy into her hand. "Let's go back out into the living room."

"Your wife did the interior design work?"

Flynn sighed. "Yes." He took a swallow of brandy as he strode back out into the front room. Once there he threw himself down onto the golden brown couch and propped his booted feet carelessly on the expensive black slate table. "Sit down."

Heather sank into the far corner of the sofa, curling her bare feet under her while she took a tentative sip of the brandy. They sat in silence for a few minutes.

"Jeremy's fever doesn't seem to be too high. It looks like what the doctor said it probably was, a stomach flu or virus of some kind."

"Yeah." Flynn gazed straight ahead at the fireplace on the other side of the room. "Sorry about the mess. Little boys don't have much self-control when they get sick."

"Hardly surprising. He's only four, you said?"

"He's just about to turn four. A few more days. The past eight months have been tough for him. First he gets swept off to California and told to call a new man Daddy, and then he finds himself back with me. It's a good thing kids are adaptable."

Heather nodded thoughtfully, studying Flynn's profile. "What about big boys?"

He shot her a brooding glance. "We're not so adaptable. Once we decide what we want we're not satisfied until we get it." He indicated the room with a slight movement of his head. "Does this bother you?"

"Does what bother me?"

"You know what I'm talking about. This house. The furniture. The kitchen. All the stuff Cheryl did to the place."

Heather hesitated and then decided there was no reason not to be honest. "It doesn't bother me exactly. But it gives me an odd feeling."

"I can't pretend she didn't exist, Heather," Flynn said bluntly.

"I know that."

"But I give you my word you can do anything you want with the house. Tear out everything and start from scratch, if you like. I never really did like most of it, anyway."

Heather looked down into her brandy. "I've got my hands full redoing my own place at the moment."

"Heather..." Whatever Flynn was going to say next was chopped off by the sound of a wail from the bedroom. Instantly he was on his feet. "Be right back," he muttered.

But he wasn't right back. Jeremy was sick again, and by the time the second mess had been cleaned up Heather and Flynn were both looking and feeling slightly frazzled.

"I have a hunch this is going to be a long night," Flynn said bleakly. "I should never have brought you here."

"We'll take turns," Heather said with sudden decision.

He looked at her as if she'd lost her mind. "Don't be an idiot. He's my son. I'll take care of him."

"A couple of hours ago you were telling me you wanted to marry me and turn me into a mother," she said lightly. "This is my chance to find out exactly what I'd be getting into if I were to accept your proposal, isn't it?"

"I wanted you to get to know him first." Flynn looked frustrated.

"You get to know someone in a hurry when he's sick, don't you?"

Flynn leaned his head back against the couch, his mouth grim. "Why do I feel as though you've done nothing but set me up all evening?"

Heather grinned ruefully. "You probably feel that way because it's exactly what I've done."

He looked at her, not responding to the laughter in her eyes. "It isn't going to be this simple, you know."

"What isn't?"

"I know why you're here. You're looking for ammunition you can use to convince yourself this whole

scene just isn't for you. You're searching for reasons
to back away from me. You think that if you take a
good look at exactly what you'd be walking into if you
marry me you'll stop wavering and decide to stay clear
of the whole thing. I know it can't be easy to come into
a home that bears another woman's stamp on every
square inch. I realize that in an ideal world you'd like
to start fresh with a child of your own rather than have
to learn to love someone else's. You've made it very
clear you'd prefer to get involved with a man who isn't
carrying around the emotional garbage of a previous
marriage. So you think that you'll plunge into the
worst of it tonight and cure yourself of any lingering
emotion you might be feeling toward me, right?''

"I don't know," Heather said with simple honesty.
"All I do know for certain is that I'm here, and as long
as I am, there is absolutely no reason we shouldn't take
turns getting up and down for your son. Now why
don't you show me to an empty bedroom?''

Flynn sat up abruptly, yanking his feet down off the
coffee table. "I'll show you to my bedroom," he said
through his teeth. "If you're so damn determined to
take the plunge all at once, you can do it right. You'll
sleep in my bed.''

Heather tensed. "Flynn, I won't go to bed with you.
I mean it.''

"Don't worry," he growled, getting to his feet.
"I've got a sick kid on my hands. Believe me, I'm not
feeling particularly passionate. Besides, the only way
we can make sure we're sharing the nursing duties
equally is to sleep in the same room. How else are you
going to know when it's your turn to clean up after
Jeremy?'' he added mockingly.

"Now listen to me, Flynn," Heather started firmly.

He cut her off with a wave of his hand. "Don't worry. The bed is huge. You won't have any trouble avoiding me. Cheryl and I shared that bed together for weeks at a time without touching each other."

It was probably that last harsh statement that made Heather close her mouth on further protest. Before she could think of anything else to say Jeremy cried out from the bedroom again.

"Your turn," Flynn drawled, his eyes gleaming with challenge.

Heather stared at him for an instant and then swung around without a word to go to Jeremy's bedside. Half an hour later, when she finally had him resettled and back into a fitful sleep, she emerged to find the living room silent and darkened. Cautiously she wandered down the hall until she found what had to be the master bedroom. It was in shadow, but she could see Flynn's sprawled form on one side of the wide bed. He had taken off his shirt and boots and replaced his slacks with a pair of jeans. He appeared to be sound asleep on top of the elegant gray bedspread.

Heather stood in the doorway, looking at him for a long moment, her thoughts turning dangerously tender. She was telling herself to find another bedroom, when Jeremy called loudly for his father.

Flynn came off the bed in a smooth rush and stood blinking for a few seconds at Heather.

"Get some rest," he muttered, and pushed past her into the hall.

Heather took a deep breath and sat down on the far edge of the bed. She might as well try, she thought. It was a cinch she wasn't going to have to worry about fighting off any passionate assaults from one Flynn Rammage this evening.

After that the issue of where Heather was to sleep became a moot point. Jeremy grew increasingly more restless. Heather changed into a nightgown and robe shortly after midnight, but Flynn didn't seem to notice or care. What sleeping he did was done in his jeans. By three in the morning they were both moving like automatons whenever Jeremy cried. Heather forgot even to think about the fact that the bed on which she was grabbing such limited rest was the same bed the unknown Cheryl had once shared with Flynn. The night became an endless series of trips to the bathroom with Jeremy, sitting by the boy's side until he fell asleep again and here and there a few minutes of rest.

Heather finally fell asleep for the last time around three-thirty. She awoke with a start three hours later, and realized the bed beside her was still empty. Flynn had never returned from his last trip to his son's room.

She sat up slowly, pulling the light robe more closely around herself. Then she stood up, yawning, and padded down the hall to Jeremy's room. There she found father and son sound asleep on Jeremy's narrow bed.

The sight made Heather smile to herself. Whatever else he was, she decided, Flynn was a good father. That was saying a lot about a man and she knew it. The world needed more good fathers.

Slowly she walked toward the bed, intending to feel Jeremy's forehead. He looked cooler this morning, she thought. But it was the warmth in Flynn's body that caught her attention as she leaned across him to put her palm on Jeremy's skin.

"Oh-oh," Heather murmured to herself, and put her hand on Flynn's brow, instead. His skin was much too warm. Flynn opened his eyes and blinked, staring up at her.

"You're hotter than a two-dollar pistol," she informed him softly. "I think you've got the same thing Jeremy's got."

"You'd better get out of the way," Flynn announced decisively. "I think I'm going to be sick." He lurched off the bed and threw himself in the direction of the bathroom.

He barely made it.

It was, Flynn decided later as he lay disgustedly in bed, not one of the finer moments in the annals of seduction.

Heather spent most of the morning moving between the sickrooms and the gleaming kitchen. In an effort to keep her patients on a steady stream of fluids she prepared tea, lemonade and milk on a rotating basis. Toward noon she started thinking about lunch, but since nobody else was she simply fixed herself a sandwich.

Jeremy, she was relieved to see, appeared to be past the worst of it. He slept for long periods until the middle of the afternoon. When he happened to wake up and find her beside him with a glass of lemonade or milk he accepted her presence without question.

"Where's Daddy?" he demanded at one point.

"In his bedroom. He's sick, too."

Jeremy nodded, looking serious. "Are you taking care of him, too?"

"I'm trying."

"Mommies are supposed to take care of you when you're sick," Jeremy informed her.

"So I've heard." Heather smiled at the intent expression on the boy's face. She could see a shadow of Flynn's adult intensity in the small features and it gave her a wistful feeling.

Ten minutes later she wandered into Flynn's room and found him sprawled facedown on the bed. He'd undressed, she discovered. His jeans were lying in a careless heap on the floor. The sheet was bunched at his waist, exposing the sleek, strong contours of his back. For a moment Heather remembered the feel of strong muscles beneath her palms and the heavy, waiting hardness of the lean, masculine body just before it covered her own.

As the image flared warmly alive in her mind Flynn sat up with an abrupt movement. He shot her an almost savage glance, and then he shoved back the sheet and swung his feet to the carpet. Naked, he padded quickly into the bathroom and slammed the door.

Heather straightened the bedding as Flynn was thoroughly sick behind the closed door. When he reappeared a few minutes later, looking wan and exhausted, she smiled gently.

"Back to bed. I've brought you some more tea. I won't ask if you'd prefer tacos or pizza for lunch." She fussed with the pillows, keeping her eyes averted from his nakedness.

"I don't think I'll ever eat again," Flynn groaned as he flopped back on the bed and yanked at the sheet. "How's the kid?"

"Asleep again. His fever's down and he's not getting sick every twenty minutes. He'll be fine. So will you in a couple of days."

"Hell. I hope you don't get this."

"Mommies don't get sick," she informed him. "They don't have the time."

"I didn't bring you here to play mommie."

"I know. You'd have preferred that I played the game under ideal circumstances."

"What a mess. You're stranded unless you call someone to come and get you. I'm in no condition to drive."

"You're in no condition to look after yourself and Jeremy, too. I'll stay. But speaking of driving, I was going to mention the subject myself."

He gave her a suspicious look. "What about it?"

"Well, I should make a run to a supermarket. We're out of milk, and I need some things for a vegetable soup I'm planning to make. Do you think you'll be okay here for an hour or so? Jeremy's sound asleep."

Flynn's brows came together in a heavy line. "How are you going to get to the store?"

"In the Porsche, of course. It's the only car around, isn't it?" She smiled winningly.

Flynn just stared at her. "The Porsche?" he finally repeated in a weak voice.

"Where do you keep the car keys?" Heather kept the bright, cheerful expression firmly in place.

"Uh..."

"Flynn, don't go all chauvinistic on me. I know you love that ridiculous car and I promise to take good care of it. I'm only going to take it to the nearest supermarket. You won't even know I'm gone."

"Well..."

"The keys?" she prompted sweetly.

"Over on the dresser," he finally told her grudgingly. He leaned against the pillows, watching with morbid fascination as she picked up the key ring he'd tossed on the polished lacquer dresser. "Heather?"

"Yes, Flynn?" She paused in the doorway with a politely inquiring expression.

"You'll be careful, won't you? Park the Porsche as far away from other cars as you can, okay? And don't try anything fancy going down the hill. You do know how to handle a gearshift, don't you?"

"I'm a fast learner," she assured him with a grin.

"Heather!"

She was gone before he could get out of bed. With a groan of despair Flynn sagged back against the pillows and closed his eyes. A man had to be strong during moments like this. When he heard the Porsche engine rumble into wakefulness outside in the drive Flynn set his teeth and endured. There were one or two shaky moments while he listened to Heather put the car into gear, and then it was all over but the waiting. She and the car were gone.

Heather did her grocery shopping with an odd sense of pleasure. She liked to cook, but other than the occasional dinner guest, she rarely had the opportunity to cook for anyone other than herself. Nothing fancy tonight, she decided as she selected fresh vegetables. Soup and biscuits would be all that either of her patients would want.

She wheeled her packages back outside into the parking lot and piled them into the Porsche. Following orders, she had dutifully parked the car some distance from the main entrance of the store. The memory of Flynn's resigned expression as she'd left with his car keys brought another grin to her face.

When she walked back into the house with her packages she found Jeremy still asleep. Heather set the paper sacks down on the kitchen counter and went to check Flynn.

"How are you feeling?" she asked, dropping the keys back onto the dresser.

"Lousy. How's the car?"

"Nice to know how your priorities are ranked, Flynn. The car is in great shape. I figure now that I've had a little practice I'll be ready to drive it into work on Monday."

His eyes narrowed. "You're staying here until Monday?"

"Unless you've got any other bright suggestions."

"I should be feeling a lot better by Monday," he said hopefully.

"I'm sure you will, but not well enough to be running around Tucson in a Porsche. Don't worry, that car and I have arrived at an understanding. How's your temperature?" She moved toward him and put her palm on his forehead. He looked up at her.

"I'm sorry as hell about this, Heather."

"You wanted me to face the reality of what you were offering, didn't you?"

"Well, yes, but not like this. Not all at once and not the worst part first."

"I figure it's kind of like you having to give me the keys to the Porsche. Shock treatment. Maybe when this is all over we'll both get cold feet and run in opposite directions."

"I won't be running in the opposite direction," he vowed. "I'll be coming after you. Remember that."

"What if something dreadful happens to the Porsche while I'm driving it?" she asked with a grin as she poured him another glass of ice water.

"In that case I'll be running after you with a vengeance," he promised. The brief flash of humor in his eyes fled before the onslaught of another wave of sickness. Flynn groaned and headed for the bathroom.

Heather wasn't sure the fragrance of homemade vegetable soup would attract anyone's attention that evening, but she was pleased to find that Jeremy, at least, was tempted. He surprised her by trailing barefoot into the kitchen, his thumb in his mouth and a ratty scrap of blanket clutched in his hand. He looked tired and slightly flushed, but his eyes were clear. He stood in the middle of the huge kitchen and watched intently as Heather stirred soup.

"Hi," he finally said.

"Hi, yourself. Hungry?"

Jeremy nodded. "Where's Daddy?"

"Still in bed. Why don't you go ask him if he's going to want any soup?"

"Okay." Jeremy turned around and traipsed down the hall. He reappeared a few minutes later.

"Well? What did he say?" Heather asked as she put biscuits in the oven.

"He said," Flynn announced as he appeared behind Jeremy, "that he thinks he can keep down a couple of spoonfuls of anything that smells as good as that soup does."

Heather swung around, the ladle in her hand. Flynn had put on his jeans and a shirt. He still looked too warm, but Heather decided he was obviously feeling stronger.

"All right," she announced as she carried soup bowls over to the glass-topped kitchen table. "Have a seat everyone."

No one but Heather ate a significant quantity of food, but she was pleased to see both males swallow several spoonfuls of soup and a biscuit or two. There was a pleasant, rather comfortable casualness around the table, and afterward Flynn and Jeremy reclined on the couch and watched television while Heather did the dishes.

"You both realize, of course, that when you're back on your feet you're expected to help with the dishes," she told them as she walked into the living room some time later. "I run a very democratic household."

Flynn looked up with a grin. "Sounds like a great incentive to stay sick."

"You have an even greater incentive to get well," she reminded him smoothly, "or have you forgotten that I'll be driving the Porsche until you're up and around?"

"I try not to think about it."

"Reality, Flynn. You must learn to face it."

He watched her broodingly that evening when she quietly made up one of the beds in the spare bedroom for herself, but he made no complaint.

By Sunday it was clear that both Jeremy and Flynn were on the road to recovery. The leftover vegetable soup tasted even better when it was reheated for lunch, and Heather decided to try solid food at dinner. She spent the day puttering around the big house, fixing snacks and drinks, playing with Jeremy and waiting on Flynn.

Jeremy was recovering quite quickly. By Sunday afternoon he was a handful as his energy returned. Never having spent much time entertaining a four-year-old, Heather was amazed at the amount of stamina required. She put him to bed that night with a sense of relief, and was startled when the boy put his arms around her neck and kissed her good-night.

"You'll be here in the morning?" he asked.

"I'll be here," she promised.

"Good." He appeared satisfied. He clutched at his blanket and watched as she walked toward the door. "It's dark," he said just as Heather started to turn out the light.

She paused, glancing back at him. "Yes, it is, isn't it? I used to be afraid of the dark, myself. I'll leave a night-light on." Matter of factly she switched on the tiny lamp near the bed, said good-night again and left the room.

Back in the living room she relaxed onto the sofa. "They certainly are lively at that age, aren't they?" she observed to Flynn, who was idly watching television.

"You learn to keep up with all that energy."

"Do you?"

He reached out to capture her hand. "Thanks, Heather. For everything. It would have been tough to manage without you."

"What about tomorrow?"

"I'll be ready to go into the office by tomorrow," he announced resolutely.

"I don't think you should. You need another day to recuperate."

"I'll be all right, Heather."

"You're not too big to listen to a little good advice. Trust me, Flynn. You need another day to recover."

"I don't...all right. If it will make you feel any better I'll phone Armina and tell her to take the day off."

"Who's Armina?"

"Armina Hodson is my housekeeper. She comes in days while I'm at work. She's been looking after Jeremy for me until I get home from the office."

"You're sure you'll be all right alone here with Jeremy tomorrow?" Heather asked worriedly.

"I'll be fine. Tuesday I will definitely be able to go back to work." He cleared his throat. "Uh, Heather, about your taking the Porsche tomorrow..."

"I can't wait," she informed him with relish. "I'm going to be the envy of all my friends."

Flynn looked at her helplessly. "Promise me you'll be careful. It's a lot of car. I don't want you taking any chances, understand?"

"Flynn, I've been driving since I was sixteen and I've never had so much as a fender bender," she told him loftily.

He didn't look particularly reassured. "Just give me your word you'll be careful. Sure you're feeling all right?"

"Just peachy. I think I'm going to escape whatever it is you and Jeremy had."

He sighed. "What a mess. I never dreamed that the first time I had you under my roof I'd be too sick to take advantage of my opportunities."

"The wonders of reality," she murmured. "I had no idea family life could be so much fun."

But when he looked at her Flynn saw she was laughing at him with her eyes. He told himself all was not lost. His hand tightened around hers.

Heather left for work bright and early the next morning in the black-and-silver Porsche. She knew Flynn was watching from the window as she pulled out of the drive, so she waved cheerily and added a small burst of rakish speed guaranteed to give him something to think about for the rest of the day.

Jeremy had kissed her goodbye, his face still sticky from fruit juice. Heather hadn't minded. She'd told him to behave himself and to take care of his father, and then, on impulse, she'd stood on tiptoe and brushed her mouth against Flynn's cheek. Flynn had been surprised by the unexpected caress. Belatedly his hands had come out to capture her waist, but he was too late. Heather was already halfway out the door.

"Well, what do you think, kid?" Flynn inquired of his son as they stood at the window, watching the Porsche disappear.

"When's Heather coming back?" Jeremy inquired, ignoring his father's more generalized question in favor of a specific one.

"After work."

Jeremy nodded vigorously. "Good. She's 'fraid of the dark, you know," he confided.

"No, I didn't know that," Flynn said musingly. "Maybe I can do something about the problem."

Heather took a detour on the way to the office, stopping by her little house to assure herself that all was well and to put on some suitable work clothes. Dressed in a snappy little red-and-white suit that she thought nicely complemented the black-and-silver Porsche, she continued on her way.

Dutifully she parked the Porsche in the farthest corner of the parking lot so it would be safe from assorted car-door disasters and then hiked for what seemed a good half mile to the main entrance of Talon and Associates.

"Hey, Heather," Terry Kent called, hurrying to catch up with her. "Saw you drive in a few minutes ago. You must have had a wild weekend to end up with a car like that."

Heather laughed. "I earned that car, Terry. I spent the weekend nursing two sick males."

Terry's eyes widened. "Two of them?"

"Uh-huh. I made hot soup, mopped fevered brows and cleaned up unmentionable messes. I was learning to face the reality of modern family life." Heather grimaced, remembering Cheryl's bed, Cheryl's kitchen and Cheryl's sofa. "How was the hot date with Lee Osborne?"

It was Terry's turn to make a face. "Let's just say I know more about his former wife than I ever wanted to know. You're right. He spends all his time talking about the divorce. When he'd finished ruining the evening with that conversation, he actually expected me to go to bed with him!"

"I thought that's where you wanted him," Heather said with a smile.

"By the time we'd dissected his divorce I wasn't in the mood."

"I know the feeling," Heather agreed in heartfelt tones. At least Flynn didn't talk any more than was absolutely necessary about his ex-wife. But Heather knew that every time she stepped over the threshold of his home she would feel the other woman's presence. Modern relationships were complicated.

Heather's particular modern relationship threatened to become even more complex late that afternoon when she hiked back across the parking lot to where she'd parked the Porsche.

The sleek rear fender had a nasty dent near the tail. Whoever had put it there hadn't bothered to leave a note.

Heather wondered gloomily just how good Flynn was at handling reality.

# Seven

Heather turned the key in the front door lock with a strong sense of doom.

"Heather!" Jeremy came running through the living room to greet her. He was obviously feeling quite normal. He wrapped his arms around Heather's legs and laughed up at her. "Daddy's fixing drinks."

Heather smiled in spite of her dark mood. "That's wonderful news, Jeremy. I'm going to need one. How are you feeling?" She stooped to give him a quick kiss.

"Feel good. Daddy feels good, too. We're gonna have hamburgers."

"One of your favorites, I understand." She glanced up and saw Flynn coming toward her. He was wiping his hands on a kitchen towel and looked as if he, too, had regained most of his strength during the day. "Hello, Flynn."

"Hi, honey." He greeted her with a possessive casualness that spoke volumes. His mouth brushed hers in a warm, firm kiss. Then he glanced down at her red-and-white suit. "I see you stopped by your house. Everything okay?"

Heather took a deep breath. "At the house, yes. Flynn, there's something I have to tell you and I would like to start by saying that it's not my fault."

His gaze narrowed for an instant, taking in the determined look in her eyes, the tension in her body and the keys dangling in her hand. He put it all together in a split second of unerring male intuition.

"The Porsche." He was already halfway out the door.

"Where Daddy go?" Jeremy watched with deep interest as his father disappeared through the doorway.

"To face reality," Heather told the boy with a sigh. "You wait here. We'll be right back." She walked out onto the front patio and stood watching as Flynn found the dent in the rear fender. He ran his hand over the marred metal as if he were touching an open wound.

"What happened?" he asked expressionlessly, not bothering to look at Heather as he examined the fender.

"I'm very sorry, Flynn. It must have happened in the parking lot. I parked it as far away from other cars as I could, but someone must have nicked it."

"This is not exactly a *nick*." The words were still curiously devoid of intonation.

Heather's chin lifted. "I will, of course, pay for the repair."

Flynn's head came up at that and he glared at her. "Paying for it is not the issue. The issue is carelessness. I warned you to be careful, Heather."

"I was careful. These things happen, Flynn. I've said I'll pay for it and I will."

"Damn it, Heather, you don't treat this kind of car the way you would that little compact you drive. Driving this car involves responsibility. I should never have let you take it in to work. I should have driven you myself. Why in hell I let you talk me into staying home today is beyond me."

Jeremy ambled outside, glancing uneasily from one adult to the other. "Daddy?" His lower lip trembled slightly.

Heather glanced down at the child and knew at once Jeremy was remembering other scenes of tension between adults, scenes that had left him with only one parent.

Flynn went toward him immediately, his voice softening at once. "Don't worry, kid. Everything's all right."

"You're mad," the boy announced with a nervous glance at Heather. "Mad at Heather."

"Yes, I am," Flynn agreed, scooping the boy up into his arms while his eyes met Heather's in a clear challenge, "but Heather's not going to run away because of it, are you, Heather?"

"Not until after I've had the drink I seem to need at the moment," Heather retorted coolly.

"Heather said you were gonna have to face re-reality." Jeremy struggled with the unfamiliar word.

Flynn arched one brow. "Did she? Well, I think I'm going to need a drink to do it."

"If the interrogation is over, I'll go change my clothes," Heather announced.

"Go ahead," Flynn murmured. "But believe me, this isn't finished yet."

"I'd like to point out that your entire case may be invalid. Somebody forgot to read me my rights." Turning, Heather walked back inside the house and headed toward her bedroom to change into jeans and a shirt. Ten minutes later she made her way to the kitchen, and found a margarita waiting for her on the butcher block island. Flynn was fixing a salad. Jeremy was nowhere in sight, but from the living room Heather could hear the sounds of *Sesame Street*. Heather picked up her drink and took a careful sip.

"So," she began with a certain defensive aggression, "are you going to skin me slowly or just tie me to an anthill?"

"I think I'll let you worry about it for a while," Flynn said as he sliced mushrooms. "But you're safe until after Jeremy goes to bed."

"I gather you don't want him watching any more battles?"

"He's seen too many."

Heather took another sip of her drink. "I really am sorry about the car."

"Don't worry, I'll find some way of reimbursing myself for the disaster." His eyes glinted for a moment as he glanced back over his shoulder.

Heather faked a small cough and said with mock formality, "Given your enthusiasm for facing the reality of a less than ideal relationship, I was hoping you'd take this little incident philosophically. As you keep pointing out, nobody's perfect, Flynn."

Flynn picked up the wooden salad bowl and came toward her to set it on the table. One brow lifted in cool acknowledgment of the small taunt. "We'll discuss the matter later."

"Will we?"

"Count on it. Now stop standing there as if you're afraid I'm going to come after you with one of the kitchen knives. Sit down and finish your drink and talk to me while I fix dinner."

Eyeing him warily, Heather slowly lowered herself into one of the steel-and-leather kitchen chairs. "If I hadn't just bashed up your Porsche, I'd enjoy this little scene. I can't remember the last time a man made dinner for me when I got home from work."

"I'm glad you're starting to see my strong points at last. And if I ever catch some other man fixing dinner for you when you get home from work I'll..."

"Daddy!" Jeremy came bouncing in from the living room.

Flynn left his sentence unfinished as he turned to answer his son. "What is it, kid?"

"Can I have a drink, too?"

"Sure. Pour the man something strong, will you, Heather? He favors apple juice. There's some in the refrigerator."

"Apple juice coming right up, pardner." Grateful for the interruption, Heather got to her feet and headed for the refrigerator.

The hamburgers were first-class. Heather was impressed and said so. Flynn appeared unexpectedly pleased by her comments. By the time all three had pitched in to do the dishes Heather was convinced the rough moments caused by the accident with the Porsche were behind her.

Under mild protest Jeremy went to bed around eight-thirty. Heather went in to say good-night and was oddly touched when she heard herself included in the boy's prayers.

"Be grateful. You may need a prayer or two later," Flynn told her blandly as he turned on the night-light and shut the bedroom door.

"Are we back to the Porsche again?"

"Not yet. Come back into the living room and tell me about your day. Just exactly how are things at Talon and Associates?"

Heather smiled. "I never discuss my company with its competitors."

Flynn chuckled. "It was worth a try. Oh, well, if you won't give away company secrets you can listen to the details of my day."

"You're really feeling back to normal?" Heather asked as she sat down in one corner of the sofa.

He nodded. "I feel fine. So does Jeremy. I'm glad to see you seem to have escaped. I suppose you'll be wanting to go back to your house tomorrow?"

"You could drive me back tonight," she observed.

"No, I couldn't," he stated positively. "I'm not feeling quite that strong."

"Flynn..."

"One more night under my roof isn't going to hurt you, Heather." He looked at her, his eyes shadowed and serious. "It's time you got used to being here."

A wave of unease swept over Heather as she glanced around the beautifully furnished room. "I don't know, Flynn," she began softly.

"Stop thinking about her," he ordered with sudden fierceness. "This isn't another woman's home. It belongs to me and Jeremy. And one of these days it's going to be your home, too. You've got to forget about the past."

"That's difficult to do," Heather said slowly. "I tried doing that eight months ago. Tried telling myself the past didn't matter. I took a chance and we both know what happened."

Flynn leaned forward, catching her face between his hands. His eyes burned down into hers. "When are you going to let that go? You're an intelligent woman. I've explained why things happened the way they did. Eight months ago you offered me comfort and compassion and love. I can't believe you haven't any left. I saw too much evidence of all three during the past three days. *Heather*." His mouth came down on hers.

She trembled under his kiss, aware of the aching intensity of it in every part of her body. Flynn crushed her gently back into the luxurious leather cushions, letting her feel the weight and hardness of his body. He intended her to know just how much he wanted her, she thought. He was counting on her responding to the desire in him. Deep down she knew she would, not only tonight but any other night he took her in his arms. The past three days had dissolved most of the barriers she had erected against him. Taking care of Flynn and his son had done what weeks of seduction might never have accomplished.

"Flynn, I shouldn't let you do this to me," she whispered huskily.

"But you will because I think you still love me a little. I'm going to make you love me a lot, Heather. Just watch." Flynn lifted his head slightly to look down into her eyes. His big hands moved carefully, cupping her face tenderly. He bent his head to trail a string of fiery kisses from her earlobe to the hollow of her throat. "Just wait and see," he promised thickly.

Heather closed her eyes, putting the past and the future out of her mind. Tonight, she vowed, would exist only for itself. Flynn was right. On some fundamental level she loved him, and she couldn't escape that fact. Tonight she would indulge that love.

Flynn felt the implicit surrender in her, and a heavy, shuddering response went through him. When he had finally found her in that cheap little house she was thrilled with he'd been certain Heather wouldn't be able to keep a lid on her passion for long. But soon after that he had begun to realize just what he was up against this second time around with Heather Devaney. Now, tonight, he was at last going to be able to pull her back into the passionate fire that had never died within him. In the morning, he promised himself, the world would be settled on its proper axis once again. Heather would be his.

"Sweetheart, you don't know how much I've wanted you." Flynn's hand went to the buttons of her shirt.

Sprawled beneath him on the sofa, her legs entwined with his, Heather whispered Flynn's name and put her arms around his neck in a gesture of feminine urgency and need that sent tremors through him.

"That's it, honey," he breathed as he slid his hand inside her shirt and found the warm fullness of her breast. "That's all I want from you. I just need to know you want me. You do, don't you?"

"I want you, Flynn. I've always wanted you."

"Oh, *Heather*."

She felt his fingertips glide over the tips of her breasts, and then Flynn moved the fabric of her shirt out of the way and lowered his head to kiss the budding nipples. Heather gasped and strained against him. The strength in him was her undoing, she thought vaguely. He coupled it with a tenderness that brought all her senses alive. She was vividly aware of the desire flaring through his whole body. The flames were leaping outward to capture and consume her.

"Touch me, Heather. The way you did all those months ago. Please touch me again."

She responded to the hoarse plea, her shaking fingers going to the buttons of his shirt. With frustrating slowness she undid them and then flattened her palms on his chest. Slowly she let her hands slide up over his shoulders. The male scent of him was an intoxicating lure that drew her like a magnet. The sleek, hard muscles shifted under her hands as Flynn moved. Heather opened her eyes in mute question.

"Not here," he whispered, getting to his feet. He reached down and picked her up, holding her high against his chest. "I want room, and there's a perfectly good bed just down the hall."

Heather stirred uncertainly, thinking of that bed he had once shared with his wife. "Flynn, I don't want to go to your bedroom."

"Hush," he ordered gently as he carried her across the living room. "Tonight we're going to exorcise a few more ghosts."

She wanted to argue but couldn't find the words. She wanted to protest, but couldn't find the logic. The heat in her veins was too fierce to battle alone. Heather admitted silently that she wanted to give herself to Flynn, and the truth was that it didn't matter now where or when or in what bed she did so. With a small sigh she nestled her head on his shoulder.

Flynn kissed her lightly on the forehead as he carried her into the darkened bedroom and settled her on the wide bed. He leaned over her, his hands planted on either side of her body. "It's going to be all right, Heather."

She managed a shaky smile. "I'm supposed to trust you, right?"

"How did you guess?" He sat down on the edge of the bed.

Heather heard the first boot hit the floor with a soft thud and then the second. The inevitability of what was going to happen flowed over her. When Flynn stood up to slide out of his shirt she watched with a sweet hunger in her eyes. His gaze never left hers as he unbuckled his belt and stepped out of his jeans. The lean, solid planes of his body brought back a flood of memories and emotions.

"Tonight," he whispered as he came down beside her, "you're not going to have time to think of anything else except me."

Heather turned to him, seeking the heat and strength in him. With slow, careful motions Flynn removed her shirt and then he unzipped her jeans. A few moments later she lay naked beside him, aware of his warm hand as it lay flattened possessively on her stomach.

"So soft and sweet," Flynn growled, leaning over to drop a small kiss in the valley between her breasts. "I could never forget the gentleness or the passion in you. There were nights when I nearly went crazy remembering."

"You should never have left," Heather murmured, spearing her fingers through the thickness of his hair.

"I know. But the past is behind us. Don't think about it. I don't want you to think of anything except the present."

He shifted, gathering her closer until she could feel the hard length of his manhood pressed against her bare thigh. The waiting power in him made her moan softly in anticipation and need. Heather wrapped her arms around him, trailing her hands down the sleek length of his back to the hard, masculine flanks.

Flynn muttered something sensual in response and pinned one of her legs with his own. He used the weight of his thigh to open her to his touch. Heather sucked in her breath as his fingers teased her into full, nerve-tingling awareness.

"Flynn!"

"I know," he muttered. "I'm about to go out of my mind, too. It's been so long since I've had you lying beneath me like this." He circled one nipple with his tongue, all the while stroking her with bold intimacy. "Can you feel how ready you are? You're turning into lightning in my hands." He found the heart of the passion flower he was exploring and Heather cried out, her body lifting against his in soft demand.

Flynn groaned and came down on top of her with a sudden, fierce urgency that would no longer be denied. "It's been so long, Heather. God, how I need you!"

She clung to him, opening herself completely as he settled between her parted legs. She felt the hard, blunt shaft begin to probe the moist petals of the flower he had readied, and then he was stroking deeply into the tight, damp channel. Heather's whole body convulsed under the impact of Flynn's possession. Her head tilted back over his arm, exposing the vulnerable curve of her throat.

"I remember," Flynn growled in taut wonder as he stilled himself within her. "It was always this way. The soft sounds you make, the way your whole body becomes tense, the way you cling as if you'll never let go." He kissed her throat and began to move against her. He felt Heather's nails sink into his skin and the small, sexy pain nearly made him lose what little control he had left. No woman had ever responded to him with this kind of sweet, honest passion. For eight long months he had dreamed of having her in a bed again, and now that the dreams were a reality, Flynn found himself glorying in the sensation. Reality was far better than the dreams had ever been.

Heather gave herself up to the primitive, captivating rhythm of passion. She held Flynn tightly as the sensual universe spun around her. Then the tension within her began to demand release. Heather felt the tiny shivers start deep within her body and ripple outward. Nerve-searing pleasure coursed through her and she tightened her grip on Flynn, her teeth nipping at the skin of his shoulder as he held her to him.

"Yes," he breathed heavily as he felt her release, "yes, my sweet love. That's what I want from you." He groaned, his hands clutching her shoulders, his lower body surging one last time heavily into hers, and then Flynn was shouting his own cry of release into the pillow beside Heather's head.

It seemed a long while later before Flynn finally shifted his weight off Heather's love-softened body. She lifted her lashes and looked at him with a strange mixture of shyness and lingering pleasure.

Flynn laughed silently down at her, the deep satisfaction plain in him. "Are you okay?"

"I think so."

"You *think* so. What kind of an answer is that?" He pretended to look offended. "Kindly consider my male ego, woman."

"Hmm. How do you feel?" Her mouth curved gently.

He kissed her slowly. When he lifted his head his eyes were gleaming. "I feel roughly the way I would if I had just discovered El Dorado or sacked Carthage."

"Oh, I see. Nothing special for you, huh?"

"There's a streak of mischief in you, lady, that's going to get you into trouble one of these days."

"I can't wait."

The quiet laughter died out of his face. "Tell me how you feel, honey."

"Isn't it obvious?"

He hesitated. "Maybe I just want to hear the words."

Heather lifted her hand to touch his cheek. "I feel as though I'm floating. You always had that effect on me. You're a fantastic lover and I'm sure you know it."

He frowned. "If you really think I'm fantastic you should realize it's only because of the way you respond to me. And you do respond to me. You'll never be able to deny that, will you, sweetheart?"

"No," she admitted. "I could never deny that."

He didn't look totally satisfied with her answers. Flynn stirred, tightening his hold on her. "Does being in this bed still bother you?"

Heather blinked, realizing this was the first time she had thought about the bed since Flynn had begun to make love to her on it. She shook her head slowly. "No, I don't think so."

He exhaled heavily. "Well, maybe that's one thing behind us." He relaxed into an amused smile. "Being the generous, easygoing soul that I am I might even be willing to put another small matter behind us tonight."

"What small matter?"

"The dent in the Porsche."

Heather responded to the sensual humor in him. "Oh? I didn't realize you considered that small."

"It's a question of perspective."

"Your perspective on the subject is changing?" she inquired interestedly.

"I find that the longer I have you lying here in a prone position the more inclined I am to view the dent with, shall we say, a certain sense of equanimity."

Heather giggled. "I had no idea you could be managed so easily. I'll have to remember that in the future."

"You do that." He pulled her more closely against him and covered her mouth with his own. "We'll see who winds up managing whom."

Three days later Heather closed a file folder on her desk and glanced at the clock. It was almost time for lunch. She expected to see Beth and Terry appear in her office doorway at any moment. But the phone rang first. Automatically she reached for it.

"Central Files, Heather speaking."

"I can't believe this," Flynn drawled on the other end. "A direct line right into my competitor's filing operation."

"Many more comments like that one and I'll begin to suspect that your real interest in me is quite mercenary," Heather retorted.

"Never. Just quit your job and see what happens. I'll still be hanging around you like a bull around a salt lick."

"What a charming image," Heather said with mocking admiration. "You always did have a way with words."

"I know," he agreed without any obvious modesty. "I'm calling to invite you to a birthday party."

"Your son's?"

"Right. Turning four is something of an event. The next best thing to turning five, probably. My folks are going to drive over from Phoenix for the day. Interested?"

She heard the unspoken persuasion behind the words. Flynn badly wanted her to agree. "What day?"

"Saturday. I thought we'd barbecue a few hamburgers in the afternoon. I'll order a cake from a bakery. Jeremy's inviting some friends."

Heather hesitated, and then the mental picture of Jeremy and his friends gorging themselves on birthday cake and hamburgers got to her. She chuckled. "All right, but forget the bakery cake. I'll bring one."

"It's a deal. As far as Friday night goes, I'll pick you up around six."

"I'll be ready." The date for Friday evening had been made on Tuesday morning when Flynn had driven her back to her own home. Heather sat for a moment, gazing unseeingly at the calendar in front of her as she thought about the way Flynn had moved so easily back into her life.

"Hey, Heather. Time for lunch. Ready?"

Heather glanced up at Beth. "I'm ready." As she got to her feet Terry Kent came hurrying down the hall.

"How are things going with Flynn Rammage?" Terry demanded as she caught up with her friends. "Another hot date this weekend?"

"Well, I've just been invited to his son's birthday party. Does that sound hot?"

Beth wrinkled her nose. "It means he's getting very sure of you. He wouldn't expose you to a four-year-old's birthday party unless he was convinced you were already in the palm of his hand."

Heather ignored the wry comment. "His parents are going to be there."

"Oh, boy." Terry grinned. "Sounds serious. Be careful, though. I had one promising relationship with a divorced man end right after I met the guy's parents."

"What happened?" Heather asked.

"My future father-in-law kept calling me by his former daughter-in-law's name. When the guy I was dating accidentally slipped and did it, too, I gave up."

"I can see where that would put a damper on things," Heather murmured.

Flynn put down the phone in his office and leaned back in his chair. Absently he tapped the end of a pencil on the desk in front of him as he thoughtfully considered the situation.

It was rather like fishing. First you dangled the lure, and then you slowly, carefully, played the glittering little fish until she was safely in your hands.

All in all, he decided, things were progressing reasonably well. Not as fast as he would have liked, Flynn admitted, but he was managing to get Heather past each obstacle as it arose. She had lived under his roof for a while, accepted his son and surrendered in bed with the same wild, sweet abandon he remembered so vividly. They had gotten through the sticky business of Heather finding herself stuck tending two sick males, and she hadn't run when he'd threatened to lose his temper over the dent in the Porsche. Flynn winced as he recalled the morning's conversation with the auto body repairman.

"What the hell happened?" the garage man had demanded as he examined the dent. He appeared personally offended by the calamity.

"Parking lot accident," Flynn had explained brusquely.

"Too bad," the man had said commiseratingly. He'd shot his client a knowing look, a man-to-man look of the sort men had traded since Adam. "You let your wife use the car, huh?"

"My fiancée." Flynn had been startled by how good the word had sounded on his tongue. The pleasure he took in it was almost enough to make him forget the cost of getting the dent repaired.

Things were going to work out.

She was still wary of him, he knew that, but the barriers were falling rapidly. He was going to be cautious but persistent from here on in, Flynn decided. He mustn't rush her, but he couldn't let up on the pressure, either. Slowly but surely he intended to enfold her in his life until she woke up one morning and realized she was inextricably a part of it.

Then he would take her out of that dilapidated little fixer-upper she'd bought and install her permanently in his home and in his bed.

Flynn nodded once to himself and went back to work, satisfied that matters were on track at last.

# Eight

# Eight

Saturday morning Heather went shopping for a birthday present. It had been a long time since she'd bought a gift for a small boy and she indulged herself by wandering through the toy departments of several different stores in a large mall.

As she examined the array of mechanized gadgets and plastic fantastic creatures offered for sale she let her mind wander over the events of the previous evening.

Flynn had taken her to a Mexican restaurant that was well-known for its atmosphere, oversized margaritas and strolling mariachi band. Heather had enjoyed herself and Flynn had been obviously pleased by the success of the evening. They had both relaxed and the conversation had flowed easily, just as it had during the affair eight months before.

When it came time to leave, Heather grew quieter, wondering if Flynn would assume he could stay the night. She knew she wouldn't offer much protest. But she had forgotten about the demands of single parenting.

Flynn had seen her inside the house, kissed her good-night with lingering regret and then informed her he had to get home early because the baby-sitter couldn't stay late tonight. Nancy was leaving early in the morning on a trip with her parents.

Having spent much of the evening anticipating Flynn's lovemaking, Heather found herself startled by the abrupt end of the date. Flynn must have detected her reaction, because he'd grinned down at her with a masculine arrogance that should have shamed him.

"Save it for me, hmmm?"

"Save what?" she'd snapped, torn between amusement and irritation.

"You know what. I want to be able to take my time and enjoy it." He cupped her face between his hands and brushed his mouth across hers. "When you marry me and move in with me we won't have to cut our evenings short," he added persuasively. "We'll have all night, every night."

Heather had widened her eyes in innocent surprise. "Flynn Rammage, you are not by any chance trying to use sex to entice me into marriage, are you?"

"Don't you know by now I'd use anything I thought would work? Good night, sweetheart. Don't forget the birthday cake. The kid's counting on it."

"I hope he likes chocolate."

"He does," Flynn had assured her. "Almost as much as I do."

Heather had gone to bed alone that night, lying awake staring at the ceiling for a long time. She didn't know if the uneasiness she felt was due to the knowledge that soon she would have to make a decision regarding Flynn's marriage proposal or because she was experiencing again that odd sensation of being watched. She couldn't even decide if the latter was connected to the former. After all, she had begun being aware of the vague feeling of being watched at about the same time Flynn had shown up in her life for the second time. It was probably some psychological reaction on her part. Something to do with the age-old business of man the hunter moving in on his feminine prey.

The imagery made her groan. Turning over on her side, Heather had told herself to shut up and go to sleep.

She'd baked the cake that morning before leaving on the shopping trip. Heather was rather proud of the three-tiered creation. It had been a long time since she'd baked a birthday cake. As she wandered down another aisle of toys she reminded herself to pick up some candles.

In the end Heather decided against any of the spectacular and inventive toys she found in the department stores. Most of them needed batteries and looked as though they'd break after fifteen minutes in the hands of a four-year-old. Besides, she had no idea what was in at the moment. She went into a bookstore, instead, and there she found exactly what she wanted. She spent a fortune on children's books before she even realized what she was doing, but as she walked back out of the shop she told herself she wasn't sorry. A kid couldn't have too many books.

Briefly she conjured up a picture of herself reading one of the stories aloud to Flynn's son. The imaginary scene was a cozy, warm one that brought her a quiet sense of pleasure. Heather hurried home to wrap her treasures and collect the birthday cake.

Flynn came around the corner of the house to greet her as Heather pulled into the drive and parked behind the Porsche. He waved with considerable enthusiasm and a measure of relief, and strode forward to take the cake from her hands while he dropped a possessive kiss of greeting on her mouth.

"Lord, but I'm glad to see you," he announced, leading the way into the house. "I've got four wild four-year-olds out on the back patio. My parents are doing their best, but it's been a while since they had to cope with a bunch of kids."

"You think I'm going to do any better?" Heather asked, laughing up at him.

"You, my sweet, can cope with anything." He set the cake down on the counter. "Come on outside and meet everyone." Flynn reached for her hand and pushed open the back door. An immediate screech of welcome greeted Heather's arrival.

"Heather! You came! Is that my present?" Jeremy raced forward, his face alight with the day's excitement.

"Hi, Jeremy. How are you? Yeah, this is your present." She handed it to him.

Flynn stepped in, saying firmly, "It goes on the table with the other gifts."

"I'll take it over there," Jeremy volunteered at once, scurrying off with the package. A handful of other youngsters gathered around him to admire and speculate on the new addition to the pile.

Heather smiled politely at the couple in their sixties who were sitting in lounge chairs. Flynn took her arm and led her forward.

"Heather, I'd like you to meet my parents. My mother, Audrey Rammage, and my father, Hugh. This is Heather Devaney."

Hugh Rammage, a strong, distinguished man who looked as if he probably played a lot of golf during the winter in Phoenix, rose to shake Heather's hand with a warm, friendly grip. "Happy to meet you, Heather. Flynn has told us a great deal about you. So has Jeremy, for that matter. I understand you're the one bringing the cake today."

Heather laughed. "Now I know why Jeremy bothered to mention me."

Audrey Rammage chuckled. She was an attractive, energetic woman with stylishly silvered hair. Heather guessed she, too, played a lot of golf. "Jeremy, like most men, has fairly simple, straightforward priorities. How are you, Heather? It's so nice to meet you."

Heather relaxed a little. She was surprised at the reaction, because she hadn't realized she was at all tense. She sat chatting with Flynn's parents for a few minutes while Flynn stoked up the barbecue coals. The children were playing a lively game that appeared to be a cross between hide-and-seek and tag that should have worn them out but only seemed to give them more energy.

"I don't know where they get it at that age," Audrey Rammage mused. "I'd pay good money for a bottle of that kind of energy today."

"I know what you mean," Heather said, watching the children. "I see now why people always say it's a good idea to have kids while you're still young."

Flynn shot her an odd glance, but it was his father who said jovially, "Look who's talking. You're hardly a candidate for a senior citizen's movie pass. You're young enough to take on the challenge of a small boy."

"Of course you are, my dear," Mrs. Rammage chimed in at once.

In spite of herself, Heather felt her cheeks turning pink. She avoided Flynn's amused glance and took refuge in the act of pouring herself a glass of lemonade. "Yes, well, here's to youthful exuberance," she murmured, lifting the glass in a mocking toast. "Shall I get the hamburger patties, Flynn?"

"Go ahead and bring them out. The sooner I get this crowd fed the better. Maybe food will slow them down."

"I'll give you a hand, Heather." Audrey Rammage got to her feet.

Heather nodded politely and led the way into the gleaming kitchen. "We might as well get the potato chips ready, too."

"I'll take care of the chips while you see to the hamburger patties," Audrey said easily. "You know, my dear, I was so pleased when Flynn told us about you. His father and I have been waiting for him to settle down and start getting serious about someone again. He's really a very domesticated sort of male, you know. The kind who prefers home and hearth. The divorce was very hard on him, and of course poor Jeremy suffered, too. It's about time both of them had a woman in the house again."

Heather cleared her throat delicately. "Divorce is never easy," she muttered into the recesses of the refrigerator as she opened the door, looking for the hamburger patties.

"How true," Audrey went on cheerfully. "We were worried about Flynn for a while. He was quite shaken up when Cheryl got custody. Went a little wild for a time." She ripped open a bag of potato chips and dumped the contents into a large bowl. "But that's all over. Luckily you're meeting him now, instead of eight or nine months ago. You probably would have gained a rather poor impression of him."

"Is that right?" Heather heard the dry note in her voice, and hoped Audrey Rammage missed it. She closed the refrigerator and swung around with a trayful of hamburger patties covered with plastic wrap. She saw Flynn standing in the doorway, and knew he had heard every word his mother had said. There was an enigmatic expression on his face.

"Don't forget the pickles" was all he said. He let the screen door swing shut.

"Uh-oh." Audrey Rammage appeared only mildly chagrined as her son disappeared. "I suppose he heard that last comment of mine. Ah, well. A mother's entitled to a little freedom of speech. Heaven knows I only spoke the truth. Have you got everything, Heather, dear?"

"I think so."

"Good. Let's get the little heathens fed so they can open the presents and get to the cake." Audrey started for the back door, glancing around the kitchen with an admiring eye. "You know, I will say one thing for Cheryl. She had wonderful taste. Isn't this kitchen lovely? And the rest of the house is just beautiful. She had a natural talent for interior design." Audrey pushed through the door and stepped out onto the patio. "It carried over into clothing, too. I never saw her when she wasn't beautifully dressed."

"Who's beautifully dressed, Audrey?" Hugh Rammage came forward to take the tray of hamburger patties from Heather's hands.

"Oh, we were just discussing Cheryl. I was telling Heather what sophisticated taste she had. She certainly turned Flynn's home into a showplace."

Flynn looked up and caught Heather's politely blank expression. His gaze narrowed. "Cheryl's taste wasn't mine," he said coolly. "As a matter of fact, I never liked what she did to this place. Heather, I forgot the mayonnaise. Would you bring it out, please?"

"Certainly, Flynn." Heather swung around and went back into the house. She knew full well the mayonnaise mission was merely a diversion. She had a hunch Mr. and Mrs. Rammage were getting a quick lecture entitled "We Don't Mention Ex-Wives Around Prospective New Wives." Heather hoped the message got across. She could think of other things she'd rather talk about than Cheryl's fabulous taste and design sense. Glancing down at her jeans and loafers, Heather wondered what Cheryl would have worn to her son's fourth birthday party.

When Heather returned from the kitchen a second time, the burgers were on the grill and Audrey Rammage looked slightly subdued but determinedly cheerful. Heather felt sorry for her. Flynn had probably been quite blunt.

The kids crowded around Flynn as soon as he announced that the food was ready. Heather watched in amusement as he organized the proceedings with a firm hand. The children responded eagerly to his direction and Heather was forced to admit the man had a talent for command. Flynn caught her amused expression just as he finished putting the last burger onto a paper plate.

"What's so funny?"

"I was just wondering if this is the way you are on a job site. You have certain distinctive organizational abilities."

"The only difference between organizing four-year-olds and organizing work on a job site is one of degree," he declared smoothly. "I'll admit my language tends to be a little rougher on a job site."

"I'll bet that's an understatement."

He shrugged as he set the adults' plates down on the table they were using. The kids were eating a safe distance away at a second table. "It's the only difference. The trick to giving orders is making sure that those you're giving them to understand you can enforce them."

Heather thought about that for a moment. "No," she said finally, "I don't think that's the trick at all. It's only part of it. There's something else involved."

Hugh Rammage looked interested. "What else, Heather?"

"Some people are natural leaders. People accept commands from them because they sense it's the natural order of things. There's an instinctive respect for leadership. When people like Flynn yell, other people jump. Why do you think the partnership between Flynn and Sam Erickson has always been so successful? Sam handles the sales end of the business because he has a talent for it. Flynn, on the other hand..."

"Gets stuck with all the yelling?" Flynn concluded for her with a sardonic expression.

"Speaking in purely business terms," Heather murmured, "it's an ideal combination. Things get done the way you want them done."

"Is that right?" Flynn asked dryly. "Maybe I should try yelling a little more in my private life and see if I can't get things done the way I want them done in that arena, too. I may have been taking the wrong approach lately."

Audrey Rammage interrupted with a small, rather uneasy chuckle. "Wonderful hamburgers, Flynn. Hugh, pass me the mayonnaise, will you?"

"Here you go, dear." Hugh handed the mayonnaise to his wife and turned to offer a platter to Heather. "Have some tomatoes, Cheryl."

*Cheryl.*

It was an accident and Heather knew it. A slip of the tongue that had been bound to happen sooner or later. Before Heather could think of a way to handle the verbal slip, Flynn was speaking in a low, cold voice.

"Her name is Heather."

Hugh blinked, taken aback. "Did I say Cheryl? I'm so sorry, my dear. Slip of the tongue. I'm so accustomed to thinking of Cheryl and Flynn as a twosome that I guess it's become a habit."

"Dad..." Flynn began through gritted teeth.

"It's quite all right, Mr. Rammage," Heather broke in to say gently. "A friend of mine warned me this sort of thing happens. What with all the divorces these days it's hard to keep the names and the players straight, isn't it?"

Flynn turned on her. "That's enough on that topic. Eat your hamburger, Heather."

She gave him an amused glance and obediently picked up her burger. Audrey Rammage rushed to fill the awkward hole in the conversation, and a moment or two later the small scene was behind everyone. It was Flynn who resurrected it sometime later as the tables were being cleared in preparation for the gift-opening ceremony.

He came up behind Heather as she dumped three plates into a garbage bag. "Sorry about Dad's slip of the tongue," he growled.

"Don't worry about it," Heather said carelessly. "A hazard of dating a divorced man. I'm told it's not a serious problem unless you start making the same slip."

"Who the hell told you that?"

"A friend at work."

Flynn put his hand on her arm and turned her to face him. His tawny eyes gleamed intently. "Believe me, that'll never happen, so stop waiting for the moment when you think it will."

"I'm not sure I understand the logic of that sentence."

"Figure it out for yourself." He put his arm around her shoulders. "Let's go watch my materialistic son open his presents."

The gifts, by and large, were a success. Most of them were the mechanized, motorized, plasticized toys Heather had seen on the shelves of the toy departments. After witnessing Jeremy's enthusiastic response to each new toy, Heather was quite prepared for his reaction to the books she had brought. They were obviously something of a letdown. Jeremy tore the paper off with great anticipation, but when he saw what was inside he lost interest. He gave Heather a childishly polite thank-you and immediately reached for the next present. The books were pushed to one side.

"Don't worry," Audrey Rammage leaned forward to say quietly to Heather. "When he wants his bedtime story tonight he'll be quite grateful for your gift. Books make lasting presents, even if children don't always appreciate them at first."

Heather laughed. "I didn't know what else to buy a four-year-old. I haven't been around kids his age very much. Maybe the cake will make a better impression."

Fortunately the cake made a terrific impression, especially after ice cream was added. The party eventually ended and the last four-year-old was picked up by a parent. Jeremy was left amid a pile of toys while Flynn walked Heather through the house to the drive, where she had left her car.

"I'll see you tonight," he told her as he held her car door.

She glanced up at him, surprised. "You will?"

"My folks are going to watch Jeremy."

"Oh."

He slammed the door shut and leaned casually against the car, his arms folded across his chest. "You could sound a little more enthusiastic."

She flushed. "It's not that. I just wasn't expecting to see you tonight."

"Got another date?"

"What if I have?"

He leaned down and kissed her through the open window. "If I believed you did, I'd tell you to cancel it, naturally." Flynn smiled at her wry expression.

"But the subject doesn't arise, does it? You don't have a date with anyone else."

"Sometimes, Flynn Rammage, you are much too sure of yourself."

He shook his head. "Only of what I want. Goodbye, Heather. I'll see you around six. Thanks for helping out today. Sorry about the various and assorted parental blunders. Mom and Dad mean well."

"I know. Just a hazard of dating a . . ."

His mouth hardened. "Don't you dare say it. Have you any idea how frustrating it is trying to fight your image of a divorced man?"

"No," Heather said honestly, "I hadn't thought about it."

"Well, try thinking about it. It might make you a little more compassionate." He stepped back from the car as she turned the key in the ignition.

That night as she dressed for the evening Heather found herself doing exactly as Flynn had instructed. She thought a lot about the relationship from his side. Flynn was sincere about the marriage proposal, she admitted as she zipped up the little black dress she had chosen to wear. She was willing to believe that much. She was willing to believe that his behavior eight months ago was an aberration caused by his anger and frustration at losing his son. She was even willing to believe that he was no longer driven by the demons that had been riding him when she'd first encountered him. He now wanted a wife and a mother for his son.

Heather acknowledged to herself that she wished she knew how much of her attraction for Flynn was based on the fact that he wanted Jeremy to have a mother. But it was useless trying to separate Flynn's desire for a wife from his desire for a mother for Jeremy. They were bound up together and if she accepted his proposal she would have to accept that fact.

Sooner or later, Heather knew, she was going to have to make a decision. Given Flynn's way of doing things, the deadline would probably fall sooner, not later.

She had survived another dose of reality today, Heather told herself. But she could forgive his parents readily enough. It must be a little awkward readjusting to a new woman in their son's life after thinking of him as a married man for so long. They had accepted her warmly, however, and the verbal faux pas were completely unintentional.

The bottom line in all this, Heather realized, was that she was in love with Flynn. What she really wanted was to be totally certain of his love for her. She'd like to know deep down that he wanted her for herself and not because he was looking for a combination wife and mother.

The doorbell chimed just as Heather finished stepping into a pair of tiny black sandals. She opened the door to find Flynn and another armful of chrysanthemums.

"I figured the others were probably gone by now," he announced, stepping into the room.

"I had to throw them out yesterday," Heather admitted. "Let's get these into some water. They're beautiful, Flynn."

"So thank me." He waited expectantly.

"You're not bashful about asking for what you want, are you?" She smiled, stood on tiptoe and kissed him.

"You don't usually get what you want in this world unless you ask for it quite loudly." He wandered into the kitchen and watched her put the flowers into jars of water. "How are the repairs going on this place?"

"Just great," she told him enthusiastically. "I had the painters in on Tuesday and Wednesday. Thursday someone examined the plumbing. He's preparing an estimate for some repairs. Yesterday someone came to measure one of the living room walls for mirrors. I think it will open up that room a lot, don't you? Next week the carpet people are due."

Flynn glanced idly around. "It's an old house, Heather. Don't put too much money into it."

Her mouth curved. "Are you kidding? I've already sunk my life's savings into the down payment."

"Did you have someone check the structural integrity before you bought the place? I don't like the looks of that ceiling and the floor's warping over there in the corner."

"Stop talking like an engineer."

"It's going to cost you a fortune to replace the appliances alone."

Exasperated, Heather shoved the last of the chrysanthemums into a jar. "I knew it was a fixer-upper when I bought it."

"It's more than that, honey—it's a disaster. If you aren't careful you'll wind up pouring more money into it than you'll ever be able to get out of it. The best thing you could do is sell it before you sink any more cash into repairs and upgrades."

"Flynn!"

He held up his hands to ward off her irritation. "Okay, okay, I'm just trying to hand out a little free advice."

She glared at him. "You're old enough to know that no one appreciates free advice. I'm ready to go to dinner."

"Yes, ma'am." He took her hand as he started for the door. As they stepped out into the balmy night he slanted her a speculative glance. "Are you really so attached to this place?"

"It's my home."

"I'm offering you a home, Heather. And before you tell me you don't want it because it was once another woman's home I'd like to point out that what I'm offering is *my* home, not my ex-wife's. It belongs to me and my son. No one else. When you move in, it will belong to you. Understood?"

"Yes, Flynn," Heather said in a subdued voice. "I understand."

"Good," he said with great feeling. "There have been times lately when I've found you rather thick-headed on certain subjects."

"Thanks!"

"It takes me by surprise, you know, because you always seemed like such an intelligent person."

"I don't know how you could have got that impression after witnessing my stupidity eight months ago."

His fingers tightened around her wrist in subtle warning. "What happened eight months ago was not a result of stupidity on your part."

"No?"

He opened the Porsche door and settled her inside. "No," he repeated just before he closed the door. "You went to bed with me because you loved me. I was the stupid one, because I didn't appreciate what I had at the time. I was too angry to appreciate anything except my own need to lash out at someone." He closed the door with a solid thunk and walked around to the other side. "There's just one thing I'd like to know, Heather," he added as he turned the key in the ignition.

"What's that?" She was tense now, her pleasant anticipation of the evening spoiled as she sensed that things were coming to a head.

"You went to bed with me eight months ago because you loved me. Why did you go to bed with me this week?"

Her mouth went dry. "Talk about loaded questions."

"Well?" He pulled away from the curb.

"You don't honestly expect me to answer that one, do you?"

"Yes. Honestly. You were always honest with me, Heather."

"It was one of the things that made me such an easy target eight months ago, wasn't it?"

"We're not talking about what happened before I went to Saudi Arabia. We're talking about this week."

"You're talking about it. I'm not."

"You can't avoid me or my questions much longer, Heather," he warned gently.

"Don't rush me, Flynn."

"I'm not. I'm merely applying steady, unrelenting pressure."

Heather groaned. "You're impossible."

He let her change the subject after that, and Heather was so grateful she became positively chatty. The evening went well, with the conversation having its usual seductive effect on Heather. There was no other man on the face of the earth who could charm her into bed with a discussion of his work or the weather, she thought in a flash of amusement as the dinner came to an end. Maybe it was the way he talked, not what he actually said, she reflected. Flynn always spoke to her as if she and he shared a unique wavelength. There was a bond between them that went beyond the verbal and made the most ordinary of conversations an extraordinary, subtle form of communication. It had always been this way between them and Heather knew intuitively it always would be this way.

She would be a fool not to marry him, she decided suddenly just as the dessert—raspberry shortcake—arrived. An absolute idiot. But some small part of her was still wary. She wasn't quite ready to take the final step.

"I want more time, Flynn," she said half an hour later as he parked the Porsche in front of her home.

He didn't pretend not to know what she was talking about. Turning off the engine, he crossed his arms on the wheel and stared out into the street. "Eight months ago you were braver."

"I was reckless."

"I'm afraid to give you too much time. You'll keep looking for reasons you shouldn't get involved with me." He turned in the seat, his face shadowed in the darkness of the car. "You took a chance on me once before, sweetheart. You've got the guts to take another."

She looked at him with mute appeal in her eyes. "I won't be rushed."

"What do you want from me?" he asked harshly. "I can't prove I'm not marrying you just to gain a mother for my son. I can't pretend I don't have a past that includes a nasty divorce. I can't guarantee my parents won't slip up now and then and call you Cheryl by mistake. I can't wipe out my behavior eight months ago. But I want you, Heather, and I'm convinced you want me. One way or another I'm going to make you give us both a chance.''

Before she could respond he was out of the car and coming around to her side. When she stepped out onto the sidewalk he took her hand and smiled down at her with sensual promise.

''There's one place you and I communicate even better than we do with words. I need another night with you, sweetheart. Are you going to deny me that much?''

She looked up at him wondering if he had any idea of how little she could deny him. ''No,'' she whispered.

# Nine

Hand in hand they walked up the steps to Heather's front door. Without a word Flynn took the keys from her fingers and inserted them into the lock. Then he was shutting the door behind them, closing out the rest of the world. He dropped the keys onto the card table beside the jar full of flowers and reached out to gather Heather into his arms.

"I know what I did to you eight months ago," he muttered into her hair. "I know you have your doubts about me now. But have you ever doubted the effect you have on me when I hold you like this?"

"No," she admitted, her head nestled against his chest. "I never doubted this part. The passion was always real."

"I should have realized what we had a long time ago," he muttered. "I was a fool to leave you."

They stood for a silent moment, letting the emotional impact envelop them. Then, with infinite care, Flynn drew Heather down the short hall to her small bedroom. He came to a halt in the doorway and smiled briefly at her narrow bed.

"This isn't the bed you had in your old apartment."

"The other one was rented. It went back with the rest of the furniture when I moved out. I bought this at a yard sale to tide me over until I can get exactly what I want."

Flynn wandered into the room, not bothering to turn on the light. In the shadows of the small bedroom he seemed very large and very male. His eyes gleamed in the darkness as he turned and sat down on the edge of the bed. He held out his hand. Heather hesitated and then went forward to let him wrap his fingers around her own. He tugged her down beside him. "Given the size of this bed, I gather you weren't planning on an active social life for a while."

She looked up at him, her face very serious. "I haven't had an active social life, at least not the kind you're referring to, since you left."

"Heather," he said in a dark, husky voice as he captured her face between his hands, "I never meant to ask or imply anything along those lines. I haven't the right and I know it."

She smiled mistily as she wrapped her fingers around his wrists. "There's been no one else since you left, Flynn. I didn't want anyone else."

"There hasn't been anyone for me, either, sweetheart. I swear it."

She couldn't suppress a wave of affectionate amusement. "Are you sure your state of celibacy for the past few months hasn't had something to do with the rather limited social life available in Saudi Arabia?''

He groaned. ''You little tease. It had nothing at all to do with that and everything to do with the fact that the only woman I wanted was you. I used to lie awake at nights thinking about you, imagining you in my bed. I thought of all the things I would say when I saw you again, ran through all the explanations and apologies I would make. But I knew that I was going to be totally dependent on your willingness to forgive. I was counting on your compassion and—'' he grazed her mouth lightly with his own ''—your love.''

Heather's eyes locked with his as the last word hung between them. She knew what he wanted, and the urge to give it to him was almost irresistible. But she faltered, unable to take the step that would put her over the edge and completely into his hands.

Instead she lowered her lashes and slid her fingers up along the length of his arms until her palms rested on his shoulders. Her mouth curved with a sweet, wistful sensuality that made Flynn's hands tighten on her.

''Ah, Heather, how did I ever get along without you?'' He leaned backward, pulling her with him until she was lying along the length of him. The skirt of the narrow black dress was hitched up above her knees. Flynn ran his palm down her back to the inviting curve of her hips. With his other hand he urged her head down to his own, taking her mouth in a heated kiss.

Heather could feel the urgency in his body. He was hard and taut beneath her, and the need in him, as always, seemed to have a direct channel of communication to all her own senses. She shivered lightly in his grasp, deepening the kiss of her own accord. Delicately she ran the tip of her tongue across his lips, and when he invited her inside, she accepted the invitation.

They clung there for a timeless moment, letting the sensual tension build. Then, with slow daring, Heather began to undress Flynn. He lay quietly watching her as she unfastened his shirt with fingers that trembled in excitement. There was a sexy, lazy curve to his hard mouth as she carefully made her way down to the buckle of his belt.

When the shirt was unbuttoned Heather glanced up into his half-closed eyes. Then she drew one nail lightly across his flat nipple. Flynn sucked in his breath. His fingers curled tightly around her arms.

"Do that again and see what happens," he suggested.

"You mean like this?"

"Uh-huh. Just exactly like that." He shifted abruptly, pinning her beneath him. "Now I'll return the favor."

The black silk whispered as he unzipped it and slid it off her body. The tiny scraps of underwear soon followed. In another moment Heather was completely naked. Her eyes veiled, her lips slightly parted, she watched his face as he moved his hand up beneath her breast. With a deliberately erotic movement that made her moan far back in her throat, he coaxed forth first one nipple and then the other. Heather twisted beneath Flynn as the budding excitement flared deep within her.

"I can't get enough of you, Heather. When you respond to me like this I want more and more of you. I'm a greedy man."

"Greedy and arrogant and demanding." She smiled up at him with ancient promise. "But maybe I'm a little greedy and arrogant and demanding, too, where you're concerned."

Flynn laughed softly and rolled to one side. He sat up on the edge of the bed and removed the remainder of his clothes with quick, efficient movements that revealed the depths of his eagerness. He came back down beside Heather, folding her close.

"Come here and make a few demands, sweetheart."

Heather complied willingly as he pulled her down on top of him again. She settled herself along his length and dropped tiny kisses into the curling hair of his chest. As she gently tantalized him Flynn took the pins from her hair. The heavy mass swung free, tumbling down around her shoulders and brushing lightly against his skin. Flynn murmured husky, heavy words of desire that were as old as time.

His hands moved more quickly on her skin now, stroking her senses to life as she continued to rain the light, warm kisses all over his body. When his fingers probed gently between her thighs, Heather flinched a little in reaction.

"Flynn!"

"Come and take me, honey. I'm waiting for you." He grasped her hips and guided her to where he wanted her.

Heather knelt astride his lean thighs, fiercely aware of the taut, waiting length of him. She gasped and closed her eyes as he eased her down. There was the inevitable instant of pressure as her body sought to adjust itself to his, and then he was stroking deep inside her warmth. Heather sighed and tumbled forward across his chest.

"So good," Flynn rasped as he lifted himself into her. "Like hot silk wrapped around me. You drive me out of my mind, sweetheart." His hands tightened on her hips as he urged her into the rhythm he wanted.

Exultant in the throes of the full realization of her feminine power over him, Heather laughed softly and deliberately fought him for control of the situation. She slowed, resisting the pressure of his hands, until he was forced to accept her more teasing rhythm.

It took Flynn a moment to realize just what she was doing. He didn't understand the resistance until he looked up questioningly into her flushed face and saw the excitement in her eyes. Then he knew exactly what was happening. He grinned faintly.

"Playing amazon?"

"Ummm." She set her teeth gently to his lower lip. "I think I like being the one in charge. Maybe I have a talent for command, too. I should develop it, don't you think?"

"I'm willing to let you practice a bit."

"Thank you. You're very generous tonight." She wriggled enticingly and Flynn caught his breath.

"But I think that's enough practice for tonight."

"I'm just getting started."

"Correction." He shifted smoothly, rolling her over onto her back. "You're about to finish."

He was still deep within her, the full force of his weight crushing her into the bedding. Heather gave up trying to play amazon and let herself melt in the hot embrace. All trace of amusement was gone from

Flynn's face now. His expression turned stark with the need that was swamping him. Heather cried out softly as she felt the answering response within herself.

"Oh, *Flynn*."

"Do you want me, sweetheart?" There was a new element in his gritted question, one Heather couldn't quite identify.

"More than anything else in the world." Her voice was a ragged, breathless murmur of sound. "Please, Flynn. Please, now!"

"Soon, honey. I promise it will be soon. But first I want to hear just how much you want me."

"You already know," she whispered, clutching at him as her senses began to clamor for release. Still he held himself in check, refusing to give her the ultimate. "Damn you, Flynn, you already know."

"I know," he agreed. "But I want to hear you say it. I need to hear you say it, sweetheart. It's been too long and I have to have the words."

"Flynn, I don't...I can't..." Her head twisted restlessly on the pillow, her tangled hair fanning out around her.

"Yes, you can, my love. Say it and we'll both be free."

She clung to him as the words she had kept locked inside for eight long months were torn from her. "I love you, Flynn. *I love you.*"

A mixture of triumph, gratitude and sheer relief made Flynn's eyes glitter like topaz. "Oh, sweetheart, not half as much as I love you." He gathered her to him and moved heavily within her.

Heather felt the tension burst into flames, heard Flynn's harsh cry of satisfaction, and then they were clinging to each other as if there was nothing else solid in the universe, while the fire ran its course. Then peace descended.

For a long while Heather watched the shadows of her room from the shelter of Flynn's arms. She listened to his breathing return to normal and ran her fingertips idly over his shoulder. His skin was slightly damp from perspiration. He was still lying on top of her.

When at last he lifted his head and looked down at her Heather could see the masculine contentment in his eyes. She knew it represented more than physical gratification.

"Satisfied?" she whispered.

He brushed his mouth lightly across hers. "Yes. Finally. It took you long enough to admit it."

"That I love you? But you already knew it."

He shook his head impatiently. "I had to hear it. I had to make you say the words so that we both could hear them. Don't you understand?"

"Perhaps."

"You've been trying to be so cautious since I returned. I've spent all my time figuring out ways to lure you into my net. Half the time my plans backfired. But you still didn't take to your heels. That gave me hope. I've been living on hope, honey. Lovers tend to do that, I guess. I couldn't believe you didn't still love me, but you seemed so determined not to admit it. You were so wary of me."

"Don't you think I had a good reason to be wary of you?"

He muttered something unintelligible and then said firmly, "It's all behind us. We're working in the present now. I love you and you've admitted you love me. Nothing else matters."

"If you say so." She smiled slightly, toying with his tousled hair.

"I say so." He disengaged himself slowly from her body and started to settle himself on his back beside her. The movement almost tipped him out of the narrow bed. Flynn scrabbled briefly to catch himself and swore mildly. "This is the first and last time we use your bed. It severely cramps my style."

"I didn't notice."

He grinned. "I'll take that as a compliment. All the same, I prefer the freedom of my own bed." He cradled her close. "And since that's where you'll be from now on out, the size of this kiddy bed won't be an issue."

Heather stilled in his arms. "Flynn, I'm not moving in with you."

He didn't move for an instant and then he levered himself up onto his elbow. "What did you say?"

She wished she'd kept her mouth shut, but it was too late now. "I said I'm not moving in with you. I can't, Flynn."

"What the hell are you talking about? Of course you're moving in with me. You're going to marry me, for pete's sake."

"I never said that," she protested uneasily.

Frustrated anger flared in his eyes. "You just got through saying you loved me, damn it!"

"I do, but—"

"But nothing. You love me. You're going to marry me."

"Perhaps. Eventually. But I'm not ready to take that step yet."

*"You love me,"* he repeated, each word underlined with unsubtle menace. "You just got through admitting it. You have to marry me."

"I said the same words eight months ago. I didn't wind up marrying you then." Heather responded to the anger in him with a rare, feminine fury of her own. "You always assume so much, Flynn. You figure that because you've made your decision everyone else has to fall in line. All right, I've admitted I love you, but that's all I'm going to admit tonight. I still have a great deal to think about regarding our relationship. I told you earlier this evening I needed time and I meant it."

He stared at her for a moment, and then he flung himself out of bed. Naked, he stood glaring down at her, his hands clenched into fists on his hips. "I don't know what kind of game you think you're playing, but I can guarantee I'm not going to go along with it. I have to assume you're doing this because you're still looking for some way to punish me. But I'll be damned if I'm going to stay here and take it. I've had enough of you trying to dance just out of reach. You've admitted you love me, but you say you won't marry me. That doesn't leave much, does it, except an affair?"

"What's wrong with that?" she asked tremulously as she sat up and reached for the sheet. "It would give us time to continue getting to know each other."

"We already know each other!"

"It would also give me time to decide if I can handle being an instant mother and a second wife."

"You know perfectly well you can handle it," he tossed back.

Her anger simmered. "It would also give me time to decide if I want to hear myself occasionally called Cheryl for the rest of my life."

"Now you're really clutching at straws and you know it."

"How would you know what I'm feeling or what I can handle emotionally?"

"I know what you're feeling and what you can handle because I love you and because I've seen what you can handle. You're not a trembling little thing who can't deal with real life, so don't pretend to be so high-strung and sensitive. You're just trying to get your pound of flesh out of me."

"That's not true!"

"It is true." He yanked on his pants and buckled the leather belt with a sharp, angry movement of his hand. "If you think I'm going to hang around here and plead with you to marry me, you can think again. I've put my cards on the table. I've been gut honest with you. I love you in spite of the fact that you're acting like an idiot tonight, and I want to marry you. That's my offer. Take it or leave it, but don't expect me to put up with any more wishy-washy answers. I am not interested in having an affair with you. I want a wife for myself and a mother for my son. Nothing less will do." He scooped up his shirt and shrugged into it. Tugging on his low boots, he swung around and headed for the door.

Heather panicked. "Flynn!"

He paused in the doorway to glance back over his shoulder. "When you make up your mind to marry me, let me know. But don't keep me waiting too long, Heather. I'm about out of patience."

Heather sat curled on the bed, clutching the sheet around her as his footsteps disappeared down the short hall. A moment later the front door opened and closed with a grim finality. Then she heard the Porsche engine roar to life. Only after the sound of the car had vanished in the distance did she get stiffly out of bed.

Slowly, every movement requiring great effort, Heather went to the closet and found a pair of jeans and a plaid shirt. There was no sense going to bed. She couldn't possibly sleep. She padded slowly down the hall into the kitchen and went through the routine of brewing a cup of tea. Her mind felt numb, but there was a suspicious hint of moisture at the corners of her eyes.

Irritably Heather brushed the back of her hand across her eyes and poured boiling water over the tea-bag in her cup. She wouldn't cry, she told herself. She would try to think, instead.

But it was hard trying to think logically at midnight, she discovered. The only words that took coherent shape in her brain were the three she had confessed to Flynn only a short while earlier.

She loved him.

She knew it and he knew it.

She would marry him. Heather had a hunch Flynn knew that, as well. But he had gotten angry tonight because she'd kept him dangling. The last of her wariness had formed a barrier she wasn't quite ready to cross.

Flynn, as usual, was way ahead of her. He knew what he wanted and wasn't about to tolerate unnecessary delay.

In all honesty, Heather admitted as she sipped her tea, she had no real reason to delay any longer. She knew deep in her heart that she and Flynn belonged together. She'd known that from the first moment she had met him. It was that knowledge that had made her so reckless in the beginning, so determined to wipe the pain from his eyes and replace it with love. She'd been sure of herself then, and deep down, she was still sure of herself and Flynn.

It was true that learning more about his divorce and the fact that he had a child had given her a lot to think about. But it was also true that she was more of a realist than Flynn had given her credit for being. She was also a born optimist. Second wife didn't have to mean second best. In this world there was no such thing as starting out with a blank slate. You always had to build on the foundations of the past.

Some pasts were just a little more complicated than others, Heather decided wryly, but that didn't mean two strong willed, committed people couldn't find a way to build something solid and lasting.

Flynn shouldn't have lost his temper and walked out on her tonight, Heather thought with a renewed flare of anger. They both knew she was on the verge of crossing the last barrier. There had been no reason to stalk out of the house and go roaring off into the night.

No reason unless you took the foibles of the atavistic male ego into account.

Two miles from Heather's house Flynn finally began to cool down and think. He drove the car on automatic pilot, sliding the engine from one gear to another without conscious thought as he stared straight ahead into the night.

He'd promised himself he wouldn't rush her, but that was exactly what he'd done tonight. What the hell

was the matter with him? He should have taken tonight's victory and been satisfied. After all, she'd admitted she loved him. There was only one more step
left for her to take. She'd cross that last threshold
eventually. He shouldn't have tried to grab her and
yank her forcibly over it.

The problem was that he couldn't take many more
days like today when something went wrong and he
was left worrying about the effect on Heather. The
stuff today had been relatively minor and Flynn knew
it, but it still made him uneasy. There had been his father's idiotic slip of the tongue and his mother's
thoughtless comments on Cheryl's taste in clothing
and interior design. Small lapses, but Flynn had
sweated blood during each one. He could just see
Heather storing up the evidence in her mind, weigh-
ing the pros and cons of becoming a second wife.

Tonight when he'd finally wrung the truth from her
he'd been so relieved to hear her put her love into
words that he'd leaped ahead of himself and demanded everything at once. Flynn set his back teeth
and called himself a few appropriate names.

He shouldn't have pushed so hard. She loved him.
With a woman like Heather love was inextricably
bound up with marriage and a home. She'd come
around eventually and Flynn knew it.

He shouldn't have rushed her.

Self-disgust washed over him, and Flynn found
himself letting the car ease slowly to the side of the
road. When it came to a halt he sat quietly for a long
moment and considered his options. He'd handled
everything with miserable stupidity. He'd better go
back and try to repair some of the disaster.

As Flynn swept the Porsche into a tight U-turn and headed back in the direction from which he'd come he wondered if Heather would dump the jar of chrysanthemums over his head when he rang her doorbell. He'd deserve it.

The knock on Heather's front door brought her head up with a sharp jerk. For an instant her heart pounded with excitement and relief. *Flynn*. He'd come back.

The knock came again, short and demanding, and Heather tipped over her stool as she leaped off it and flew to the door.

"Flynn! Thank God, you came back." The words tumbled forth as she swung open the living room door. They died on her lips as she stared in horror at the strange man standing on the front step.

He was young, probably about twenty-three or so, with long, lank, blond hair that looked as though it hadn't been washed in several days. The stranger was thin, his features sharp in a gaunt face. His pants rode low on narrow hips. His clothing was old and dirty and there was a haunted, desperate expression in his faded blue eyes.

None of that bothered Heather nearly as much as the gun in his hand.

"What do you want?" she managed in a tight voice, not daring to move.

"Get out of my way." He stepped into the tiny hall, jerking the door out of her hands and slamming it shut behind him. "Go on, get back. Get out of my way."

The adrenaline of fear poured through Heather's veins. She stepped backward carefully, shaken by the desperation in the man. "Tell me what you want," she tried to say soothingly.

"I want the money. What do you think I want?" He darted a nervous glance around the room. "I know it's here somewhere. I know it. He hid it here before the cops got him and I'm going to find it. It belongs to me. *Me.*"

"I don't know what you're talking about." Heather continued to back away from the gun. "I have some money in my purse. Not much. Take it and get out."

"*Shut up.* Just shut up, you bitch." There was an almost hysterical note in his voice. "I don't give a damn about your money. I want the stuff he hid in here."

"Who hid it?" Keep him talking, Heather told herself. Maybe if he talked long enough she could think of something intelligent to do.

"Beckler."

"Beckler?"

The young man gave her a furious look, as if he blamed her personally for what had happened. "Beckler and me were partners. We pulled that job together. Then the cops came and we had to split. He had the money and he hid it before they got him. I know he hid it, because they never found it on him."

"I see." Heather licked her lower lip. "Where's Beckler now?"

The man lifted one shoulder carelessly. "Doin' five to ten. But I know he got rid of that money before they got him and I know he hid it here. He told me before the job that we could stash the money here in the house. I couldn't get back here until a few days ago. Then I find out the place has been sold and you're busy movin' in. Every day there was someone here. Electricians, you, repairmen. I got in one afternoon, but I didn't have time to do much lookin' around. I finally decided to try again one night while you were out with some dude in a Porsche. But you came back before I'd even started looking. Then the cops came. I had to lie low for a while. Always something, damn it. Always something getting in my way."

Heather remembered the eerie sensation of being watched. She shivered. "But where did your friend Beckler hide the money? This place was completely empty when I moved in, I swear it."

"The wall, I think," the young man said, his eyes narrowing. "I been thinking about it, and it's got to be somewhere in the walls or maybe under the floor. He said he'd hide it inside the house itself where nobody would ever find it. *I'm going to find it.*"

"You'll have to tear up the whole house in order to look for it. You can't do that. What will you use for tools?"

"I'll find something," he muttered sullenly.

"This is crazy," Heather whispered. So was he, she thought on a wave of panic. This fool in front of her was nuttier than a fruitcake. *And he had a gun.*

"I'm gonna find that money!" he blazed. "It's mine. Beckler can't use it. He's in jail. That money is mine."

Heather put out her hands in a calming motion. "All right, all right. I'll help you look. I want you out of here as soon as possible, so I'll help you look."

He stared at her. "I thought that guy in the Porsche was gonna stay the night. I was gonna come back again tomorrow night. But when I saw him leave I figured this was gonna be the best chance I'd get."

Heather nodded. "Yes, I can see that. Where do you want to start looking? In here?" She stared helplessly at her newly painted living room walls. "How about the hall closet? That seems like a logical place to start, doesn't it?''

"Shut up, bitch." His eyes narrowed. "I don't trust you."

"The feeling is mutual. Listen, I only want to get this over with as soon as possible. I won't give you any trouble. I swear, I'll just help you look and then..." She broke off as the sound of a familiar engine sounded out in the street. Flynn's Porsche. He'd come back, after all. Heather was torn between a new fear and an overwhelming sense of relief. *Flynn had come back.*

"What is it? What're you lookin' so funny for?" the man with the gun demanded just as the front door-bell chimed. He spun around and stared at the door. "It's him, isn't it? The dude in the Porsche."

Heather said nothing, holding her breath. Flynn rang again.

"Heather? It's me. Open the door. I've got to talk to you."

The intruder jerked around to confront Heather, his eyes wild. "Get rid of him. You hear me?"

"I hear you."

Heather walked slowly across the room to open the door. She eased it open a couple of inches and met Flynn's glittering gaze through the crack. "Flynn."

"Let me in, honey. We've got to talk."

Her throat tightened. "I can't. Not now. Go away, Flynn."

Flynn heard the words, but his whole attention was on the silent message in her eyes. He realized she was terrified. All the avenues of silent communication that existed between them were wide open, and pulsing with warning.

"Heather, what's wrong?"

"Please go away, Flynn. I can't talk to you tonight."

"The hell you can't." Quite calmly Flynn hooked his hand around the door and pushed it inward with inexorable power.

He stepped into the hall and came face to face with the man holding the gun. Flynn sighed. "Christ, Heather. I leave you alone for five minutes and you get into trouble."

## Ten

# Ten

Who the hell are you?'' Flynn asked very gently. The young man standing in front of him looked far too nervous for anyone's peace of mind. Too bad there wasn't someone around with a bottle of tranquilizers. This guy needed something to stop the trembling in his fingers.

"None of your damned business. I told her not to let you in here. I told her!"

"I didn't give her much choice, did I? It's all my fault. Now would you please explain what's going on here?" Flynn took a casual step forward into the room. Instantly the intruder lifted the gun in warning. "Watch it. Just stay where you are while I figure this out. I gotta think."

It was Heather who answered Flynn's question. "He's come for the money his partner apparently left somewhere in this house. He doesn't know where it is.

He's been watching the house, waiting for a chance to look for it."

Her tone of voice was almost conversational, Flynn noted. She appeared very calm, almost relaxed. Only the unnatural brilliance of her eyes betrayed her tension. After one assessing glance Flynn didn't look at her again. He concentrated on the man with the gun. The guy was scruffy, scared and riding the last of his nerve. It was a dangerous situation, but it was also one that might offer a chance.

"You were the one going out the back door as we were coming in the front the other evening, weren't you?" Flynn asked casually.

"You shouldn't have come back when you did. I needed more time. You shouldn't have come back tonight, either. That money is mine."

"I'm not arguing about it."

The gunman was trying to cover both Heather and Flynn simultaneously. The nose of the weapon swung jerkily from one to the other.

"You're in my way. Both of you," the stranger announced. He sounded both hurt and furious, as if he suspected Heather and Flynn had deliberately set out to make life difficult for him. "You shouldn't have gotten in my way."

"We'll be glad to get out of your way," Heather assured him briskly. "Believe me, we're not any happier about this than you are."

The young man glared at her, wiping his mouth with the back of his free hand. His eyes darted back to Flynn. "I've got to get rid of you now. You see that, don't you? I don't have a choice, do I? You've both seen me. You can identify me."

"But we won't," Flynn said, lying easily. "Will we, Heather?"

"No," she agreed. "You're welcome to search the house. We'll be glad to get out of your way, or we'll help you look for the money if that's what you want."

"You think I'm stupid, don't you?"

"No, we don't," Heather tried to say, but the gunman wasn't listening.

"I'm not, you know. It's my partner who's stupid. He's the one who's in jail, you see. I'm free. He always thought he was so smart, but look where he is now."

"A good point," Flynn acknowledged seriously.

"That money is mine!" The nose of the gun jerked authoritatively again. "Get closer together. Come on," he added to Heather, "go stand next to him."

"I don't think that's such a good idea," Flynn said thoughtfully. "Stay where you are, Heather."

The intruder's face contorted into a snarl, and for an instant Flynn was afraid he'd gone too far, too fast.

"I give the orders around here," the man shouted. "I want her next to you so I can keep an eye on both of you at the same time."

"And I want her to stay where she is. If you're going to kill us you can't expect us to make things simple for you." Flynn kept his voice quiet and soothing but filled with a reassuring authority. He'd used this tone more than once in difficult situations on a job site. He tried another step closer, keeping the movement as unthreatening as possible. "Take it easy now. There's no need for any of this. You're a smart man. You said so yourself and I believe you. If you weren't, you'd be in jail like your partner. As for Heather and me, our only interest in this is staying alive. You're right about the money being yours. We don't want it. But I don't think you want any more trouble than you've already got. We're willing to cooperate, and right now our cooperation could help you a lot."

"One more step and I'll pull this trigger."

Flynn shook his head as if giving the matter careful consideration. "That would be a mistake. The sound of a gun going off will alert the neighbors, won't it? They'll call the cops and the authorities will be here before you've had a chance to begin searching the house. You'll never get your money that way."

"Shut up, damn you! I gotta think."

"Flynn has a point," Heather observed. "You can't risk killing us now. Not if you want to take your time searching for the money. If you're really determined to look for it, I can help. After all, I've been over this place with a fine-tooth comb more than once during the past few days. I just bought this house, you see. Naturally I went through it thoroughly deciding what repairs and modifications to make. There were one or two things I happened to notice. They didn't mean much to me at the time, but..." She halted, frowning thoughtfully.

"What the hell are you talking about?" the gun-man rasped.

"Well, there were a couple of odd marks on the walls. I had them painted over. I assumed they were just some kid's doodles. You know how kids are when they've got a pack of crayons and a nice wall. But they were rather strange marks, now that I think about it. You don't suppose your partner was trying to mark the spot where he hid the money, do you? I could show you where they were before the painter covered them."

"*Shut up!* Let me think, damn it."

Silently Flynn wished him good luck in the endeavor. He doubted the gunman had had too much experience in thinking clearly. He eyed the man's grip on the gun, judging distance and the level of anxiety that was dominating the man's actions. Construction bosses tended to develop a rough-and-ready version of practical psychology.

"I know what I'm gonna do," the intruder announced triumphantly. He scowled at Flynn. "I'm gonna tie you up. You're the one I gotta watch. You might try somethin'. So I gotta put you out of commission while I look for the money. The broad can tie you up and then she can show me where those marks on the wall were. I can kick a hole in that wall easy enough. Yeah. That's what I'll do. Afterward I can figure out what to do with the two of you." He appeared considerably cheered by his own decision making. His gaze darted toward Heather. "Come here."

"Why?" she asked with what Flynn thought was remarkable politeness.

"Just keep your mouth shut and come over here!"

"Okay." Slowly Heather took a few steps toward the gunman.

When she was almost within reach the man leaned forward and grabbed her arm. He yanked Heather in front of him and put the mouth of the gun against her throat. Heather sucked in her breath, but she said nothing. Her eyes met Flynn's.

Flynn stifled a savage oath.

The gunman was pleased with his ploy. He looked challengingly at Flynn, as if checking to be sure the other man appreciated the brilliant strategy. "One false move from you and she gets it. Understand?"

"I understand."

"Stay right where you are while I figure out how we're gonna do this. We need some rope or some-thin'."

"I've got some heavy twine in the kitchen," Heather volunteered softly. "In one of the drawers near the stove."

"If you're lying, I'm gonna kill him first and then I'll kill you."

"I'm not lying."

"All right. We'll all move into the kitchen so's I can take a look in that drawer." The intruder started moving backward toward the kitchen doorway. He dragged Heather with him and nodded at Flynn. "Now it's your turn. Move real slow but keep up with us. I don't want you out of my sight."

"Sure," Flynn said.

In a stately procession the trio began to move to-ward the kitchen door. Flynn didn't take any more steps than the gunman did, but he tried to cover more ground with each one. It wasn't all that difficult be-cause Heather was making her captor's progress dif-ficult. She wasn't struggling overtly; she was simply letting her weight and the natural tension of her body make things awkward. She stumbled a little and the gunman swore. Slowly the gap between Flynn and the desperate young man narrowed.

Heather was doing her best to make her actions ap-pear cooperative, without actually contributing to the progress toward the kitchen. She could feel the al-most rigid anxiety in the man who held her. The arm he had wrapped around her waist was stiff with ten-sion. He was breathing too quickly and there was an acrid odor of sweat emanating from his body.

But the most important sensation she picked up was that the intruder didn't really seem to fear her. She was a nuisance to him, but it was Flynn's presence that alarmed the gunman. The proof of that lay in the fact that the nose of the gun kept slipping from her neck to point toward Flynn. When she looked into Flynn's eyes she knew the man with the gun was right to be alarmed. Flynn was waiting for an opening.

"Watch it," the man ordered as he dragged Heather to a point alongside the rickety card table. But the warning was meant for Flynn, who was gliding forward in a movement that left him almost within striking distance. "Just watch it. Don't get too close, you hear me?"

"I hear you."

Heather's attention was on the mass of yellow chrysanthemums filling the corner of her eye. She was only going to get one chance. She had better make it good, or both she and Flynn were going to become victims.

She was relying on the nervous tension in her captor to render him more clumsy than he might be under normal circumstances. As for herself, she wasn't too worried. She was already frightened enough to make her very clumsy. The first faltering step must appear natural. Deliberately she let her foot tangle with the leg of one of the folding chairs near the card table. There was a sharp, clattering sound and the gunman jumped.

"Watch your feet, you fool," he snapped at Heather.

"I'm sorry," she muttered, still trying to recover her balance. She flung out her arm as if to steady herself on the back of the chair, but her hand swept against

the flowers, instead. The jar of water and chrysanthemums toppled heavily onto the table and promptly
began to roll toward the edge.

"What the hell's the matter with you?" The man
jumped at the new sound, still trying to steady his
captive with his free hand. He tried to haul her back
against him, but she was clutching at the edge of the
card table now. It tilted quickly beneath her weight,
accelerating the jar.

As the glass jar full of flowers crashed to the floor,
the table collapsed. Simultaneously Heather's foot
tangled with one of her captor's.

Everything happened at once. The gunman panicked and grabbed again for his human shield. His
concentration slipped from Flynn for a few vital seconds. The clatter of falling card table, jar and flowers
was a distraction that his high-strung nerves couldn't
handle.

Flynn was on the man before the table hit the floor.
There was an ear-splitting crack and the gun bucked
spasmodically in the assailant's hand. It was followed
by a scream of anguished rage that was cut off
abruptly as Flynn drove the gunman to the floor.

Heather jumped out of the way, watching anx-
iously as Flynn made short work of his opponent.
Without the gun, the younger man didn't stand a
chance. The years of ramrodding construction work
in the field had left their mark on Flynn. He had the
coordination and muscled weight to wrestle the intruder to the floor. He also had the ruthless fury to
knock the man unconscious as he overpowered him.

The gunman made a few frantic efforts to claw
himself free of Flynn's assault, but the effort was useless. In a matter of moments the stranger was lying still

on the tattered carpet. Blood trickled from the corner of his mouth.

"Flynn! Are you all right?" Heather touched his shoulder.

Still astride his opponent, Flynn looked up at her. Heather caught sight of something very cold and very dangerous in his eyes before it began to recede from the tawny gaze. For an instant she was looking into the eyes of a primitive warrior whose blood still pulsed with the excitement of the hunt, and then Flynn blinked slowly.

"I'm all right." His breath began to return to normal as he got to his feet. He stood facing her, his intent gaze raking her from head to foot. "What about you?"

"I'm fine." Heather tried a rather shaky smile, and then with a low exclamation of relief she hurled herself into his arms. "Oh, Flynn, I knew you would come back tonight. I knew it."

"Eight months ago you should have known that sooner or later I'd come back," he said thickly into her tousled hair as he wrapped her close against him.

"Well, that makes us even. You should have known when you stomped out of here tonight that I was going to marry you."

"Heather." His arms tightened. "Are you sure?"

"Do you doubt it?" She raised her luminous eyes to meet his.

He stared down at her. "No," he said after a moment. "But sometimes it's reassuring to hear the words."

"I know."

* * *

"I don't get it," Beth Montgomery stated Monday at lunch. "How did the police know to look under the warped floor in the kitchen to find the money?"

"Because that's where Flynn told them to look," Heather explained patiently. "When he went through the house with the cops he could tell someone had recently fooled around with that section of the kitchen flooring. He pried it up for the police and there it was—the money that had been missing since that big department store robbery last June. The guy who hid it there had been renting the house before he pulled the robbery. He hid the cash there when he realized he was a suspect. He went to jail without revealing the hiding place, but his partner, who was picked up on another charge shortly after the robbery, eventually came looking for the loot. By then I was in the house. Things were busy during the day while I was at work because I had so many electricians, painters and repair people going in and out. The partner tried to go through the place on a couple of occasions when there was a break in the traffic, but he got scared off both times when I came back unexpectedly." Heather remembered the telltale footprint she'd found in the walk-in closet. "Eventually he got desperate and decided to enter the house while I was there. On Saturday night he waited until Flynn had left, and then he came to the door with a gun. Unfortunately for him, Flynn came back."

"Lucky for you," Terry Kent breathed, shaking her head at the close call.

"Ummm, yes," Heather agreed with a small smile.

"You didn't know a criminal had been the last tenant in your new house?" Beth asked.

"Are you kidding? What seller is going to tell a prospective buyer a thing like that? I knew the house had been a rental, but that was all I knew. That's the thing about buying a fixer-upper, I suppose. All sorts of surprises."

Beth raised one eyebrow. "Not much different from marrying a man who's been divorced and is raising his own kid. All sorts of surprises. You sure you want to go through with this, Heather?"

"I'm sure." She had been all along, Heather realized. She just hadn't been ready to admit it.

"When's the wedding?" Terry asked. "I want to be there."

"Don't push her, Terry," Beth admonished. "She's probably not going to have a large, full-scale wedding, anyway. Isn't that right, Heather? After all, Flynn's already had one of those. No man wants to go through the big production twice."

"But it's Heather's first wedding," Terry protested. "With any luck, it'll be her only wedding. She deserves all the trimmings. Don't let anyone talk you out of it, if that's what you want, Heather."

Heather glanced up from the taco salad she was devouring with enthusiasm and saw Flynn approaching the table. She knew he had overheard the last few comments on second weddings. "I was planning on keeping it small," she said with a smile.

"Heather can have any kind of wedding she wants," Flynn informed everyone at the table. "I don't give a damn as long as she marries me." His eyes met Heather's with absolute assurance.

Terry went pink with embarrassment and hastily changed the subject. "What are you going to do with your house, Heather?"

Heather's gaze was still locked with Flynn's. "Put it on the market or turn it back into a rental. I haven't decided yet."

"I'm going to help her get it into shape," Flynn said. "I've had a little experience with construction work."

Beth laughed suddenly. "So I hear. Best of luck to you both. I hope you'll be very happy."

"Thank you," said Heather as she got to her feet. "And don't worry, you'll both be invited to the wedding, regardless of how small it is."

"Good," said Terry. "There's something nice about weddings, even if half of them do end in divorce. Sort of a ray of hope in the darkness."

"This wedding," Flynn informed her with absolute certainty, "isn't going to end in divorce." He took Heather's arm.

"See you tomorrow," Heather said to her friends.

"Where are you going?" Terry demanded.

Flynn laced his fingers possessively through those of his future wife. "Didn't she tell you? She's going to take the afternoon off to go furniture shopping with me."

"We're going to redo Flynn's home," Heather explained, laughing. "Every single room."

"Wow!" Terry's eyes widened. "That'll cost a fortune."

"Worth every penny," Flynn assured her. "Ready, honey?"

"I'm ready." And she was, Heather knew. Ready for the new future she and Flynn would create together.

*Silhouette Brings You:*

## Silhouette Christmas Stories

Four delightful, romantic stories celebrating the holiday season, written by four of your favorite Silhouette authors.

**Nora Roberts**—*Home for Christmas*
**Debbie Macomber**—*Let It Snow*
**Tracy Sinclair**—*Under the Mistletoe*
**Maura Seger**—*Starbright*

Each of these great authors has combined the wonder of falling in love with the magic of Christmas to bring you four unforgettable stories to touch your heart.

Indulge yourself during the holiday season...or give this book to a special friend for a heartwarming Christmas gift.

**Available November 1986**

XMAS-1

**Available
October 1986**

# California Copper

The second in an exciting new
Desire Trilogy by Joan Hohl.

If you fell in love with Thackery—the
laconic charmer of *Texas Gold*—you're
sure to feel the same about his twin
brother, Zackery.

In *California Copper*, Zackery meets the
beautiful Aubrey Mason on the windswept
Pacific coast. Tormented by memories,
Aubrey has only to trust . . . to embrace
Zack's flame . . . and he can ignite the fire in
her heart.

The trilogy continues when you
meet Kit Aimsley, the twins' half
sister, in *Nevada Silver*. Look for
*Nevada Silver*—coming soon from
Silhouette Books.

DT-B-1

# FOUR UNIQUE SERIES
# FOR EVERY WOMAN YOU ARE . . .

## Silhouette Romance

Heartwarming romances that will make you laugh and cry as they bring you all the wonder and magic of falling in love.

*6 titles per month*

## Silhouette Special Edition

Expanded romances written with emotion and heightened romantic tension to ensure powerful stories. A rare blend of passion and dramatic realism.

*6 titles per month*

## Silhouette Desire

Believable, sensuous, compelling—and above all, romantic—these stories deliver the promise of love, the guarantee of satisfaction.

*6 titles per month*

## Silhouette Intimate Moments

Love stories that entice; longer, more sensuous romances filled with adventure, suspense, glamour and melodrama.

*4 titles per month*

SIL-GEN-1A